Viking
Killing the Young

A Saga

By

Michael de Angelo

Gododdin Publishing
San Francisco ~ London

First Printing 2009

For the strength of the children...

VIKING

KILLING THE YOUNG

KONGERIKIT NORGE

A. D. 99ᴆ

"THE WARS HAD BEEN
LONG, THE SAILINGS LONGER..."

CHAPTER ONE

HOMECOMING

Closer to home each pull of the oars brought him as their shield-adorned longship cut though the cobalt waves. The great goatskin drum's thunder challenged the churning seas and boomed down upon the shoulders of his battle-weary hearth-companions beating their oar blades. Over the gunwales, the blue seawater splashed and wet his lips with bitter salt as the great oak mast above creaked and pitched in the fierce white-haired sea.

Pulling to the drum's steady beat, Gundar counted his each hundred strokes. His muscles burned like forged metal while the freezing teeth of the great North wind snapped at the red and white striped sail and whispered warnings of waiting wet death below.

The wars had been long, the sailings longer. The smell of the seas lived in his lungs. Endless battles rang loud in his mind, not yet over, never left behind. Three years or four, half his hearth-companions were gone. They had paid the price in blood. Only twenty men now heaved the oars beneath the iron-nailed dragon's head fighting through the seas.

Their ship rode low in the waves, laden with the hard won treasures of their plunder, copper, silver, and bronze, but he cared about only one. At his feet, sealed in a pouch of waxed hides against the sea's splash, were the precious scrolls.

He had found them beneath an altar of the new and strange religion where his companions had left them after tearing down an altar looking for gold underneath. Only Gundar, from the moment they were uncovered, had sensed their power.

He had taken them and guarded them ever since. At the next village they had raided, while his hearth-companions plundered and took women at their will, he had searched out an oracle to make the marks of the scroll speak. The oracle's words were not what Gundar had expected. He warned him the scrolls would lose him his place with his ancestors in Valhalla, and destroy any favor the gods might grant him while on earth. Still, he held onto them, not wanting to believe the words of the oracle, hoping there was more.

When he glanced down at them, Uffi, called Anvil-head, seated on the rowing bench across, noticed.

"New Gods anger the old, Gundar," Uffi tossed out.

"You'll lose your place at Odin's table," Armod War Tooth joked.

"Unless he can see with two eyes what Odin cannot see with one," Uffi added.

Gundar played along, knowing the men needful of any fellowship now. "So I will, once I make their marks speak."

"Myself, I think the altar stones more valuable," Ingvar Long Reach contributed.

"Maybe he can turn that paper into gold at the time of the Wergild," tossed out Owen the Bald.

The men laughed as they pulled on their oars.

"Then buy passage on the ships of Asgard to escape the twilight of the gods!" joked Airik.

"Or storm the gates of Valhalla," added Hadd the Grim.

Gundar, listening with good spirit, smiled and answered. "Valhalla. Where I'll be bending Odin's ear, with a word on letting the likes of you feast at his table!"

All laughed again, and their laughter was like water on parched throats, after their many losses and hardships.

The great drum stopped. The men shipped their oars, each man retreating into the private rhythm of his own heart and thoughts. Everything that could be said amongst men had already been said, through bloody battles and long voyages over cold windblown lands and angry seas.

Now instead, they began to think of the loved ones they hoped would be waiting on the far shore. In that longing reverie, amidst those better memories, another image appeared, less real, and more. Through the floating mists, as they passed the jutting point of land, a ship appeared by the shore. It lay anchored by the village they had raided two days before. Plumes of black smoke were still rising into the sky. The men shipped their oars to glide silently past, watching with reverence the ancient burial ritual.

They knew on the funeral ship was the body of Aleric, the chieftain Gundar had slain in battle only days before.

Two armored warriors were lifting a grey-haired woman in ceremonial dress high above the heads of the warriors. It was the chieftain's wife, who would travel with him to the other worlds.

"You have made his road to Valhalla, Gundar," Uffi said.

As Gundar watched, ten fine horses were led onto the ship, to burn with their lord. He could hear the funeral rites in his mind. For each time the chieftain's woman was lifted up and down, she would be reciting the ancient chant:

3

Lo, there do my eyes behold my father and my mother,

Lo, there do my eyes behold my sisters and my brothers,

Lo, there do my eyes behold the great line of my people back to the beginning...

And Skuli, in perfect rhythm added aloud, "I hear their voices calling me, to claim my place among them in the long halls of Valhalla, where the brave do live forever."

They put her on the funeral ship, and threw a hundred torches upon it. Gundar and his companions watched without words as they pushed it off into the waves and it exploded into a tower of flames reaching skyward.

"The skein of Aleric's life is tied," Uffi said.

"The woman he once chose now chooses him," Arnod added.

Gundar saw Aleric's face clearly in his mind, a man he had known since he was a boy. He looked down at his hands, hardened and strong. They had been different when he met her those many years ago. Helga...he was eighteen, she, sixteen. He had met her at the time of the Wergild.

How he remembered that day. Amidst the feasting and the lawgiving, the judgments and the games, he had seen only her. She had eluded his gaze, pretending not to notice. Yet they both knew, and they had never stopped knowing since that day.

He wondered about her beauty now...she would be a woman, no longer a girl.

That Wergild time was like every other, like many he had attended before, but for him and Helga, unlike any other.

"To order! To order!" A voice rang out over the crowd.

Ogurr the Fearless pounded on the great oak table with the butt of his battleaxe. He sat with the elders of the nine villages, who were the lawgivers and judges.

"To order! To order!" he shouted, with little effect.

Gundar watched him, amused, wondering what he would do next to enforce his will. It was always the same. The crowd continued to roar. Children in tawny wraps and leather thongs ran and laughed. Traders bartered loudly at oak tables, and pigs and goats mingled loudly with the throng. People danced, and the music did not stop. This was his eighteenth year at the annual Wergild time. He remembered almost all of them.

"To order!" Ogurr roared again.

Still, the boisterous crowd ignored him. Standing to his full height, Ogurr heaved his axe high above and toward the crowd. A shout went out, a cry and warnings, and the crowd split and silenced as they watched the giant axe part the sky in a great arc and fall amongst them.

Ogurr smiled, remarking wryly, "The gods give thanks for you for your attention."

Everyone laughed.

He continued, "This is the four-hundredth year of our Wergild in these parts, and in the tradition of our forefathers, the elders will mete out justice that there might be peace amongst the families and the villages."

It was then that he had first seen her. That day, the sea was crashing hard, wind-driven, against the cliff below. The sun was bright and shining on her fine yellow hair that the wind floated in wisps about her head. She moved as a soft wind through a sail, with playful grace, yet still certain of her movements. She had seen him, too. He had slipped through the crowd catching glimpses of her, while she saw him without meeting his eyes, and the feasting and revelry continued all around....

Her beauty had captured him, her hands, fine but not delicate, perfectly turned, with smooth fingers that moved gracefully through the air, her eyes, so bright, with wisdom that always seemed to know, her lithe movement, with long, lean and strong limbs. The features of her face were flawless, perfectly composed, balanced in a way that pleased the eye and the mind.

The elders and the lawgiver droned on...

"Then Sverri, nine years old, son of Ulfen, went across the stream, and struck off the head of Eykr, eight years old, son of Petrus.

"...a boy, not yet a man, but yet of fighting age."

"It cannot be the full Wergild," said one.

"Nor that for a child," countered another.

"It should be half then," resolved another.

"Half then." The matter was settled.

The elders nodded amongst themselves.

The eldest spoke. "So be it then. Ulfen Arnason will pay to Petrus Haroldson a Wergild of four cows for his son striking off the head of young Ekyr."

The crowd nodded its approval. The killing tax had kept the peace amongst the villages for ten generations, but that day none of it mattered to young Gundar. He had found the woman he would marry, the woman of his bed and hearth who would bear his children.

Behind them on the shore, the funeral ship turned into a great funeral pyre of thirty-foot flames. The drum began again, and his hearth-companions began to row.

Gundar picked up his oar and joined them, thinking still of Helga. Since that time, there had been so many moments, of laughter, of joy, when the brightness of her eyes had filled his heart, of quiet desire, when the strength and grace of her limbs had filled his mind. It would always warm him, to think of her.

He remembered the last time he had seen her, three summers ago, when she had seen him off on this voyage. She had been holding their six-year-old son by the hand and cradling in her arm their two-year-old daughter.

The ship glided on through the waves that splashed in a steady rhythm against its wooden planks. It had been nine years since that Wergild.

"Gundar?" It was Skuli Ironside, holding out a wooden cup of water. Gundar looked up. Skuli was not tall, but as broad as a bull, and could throw a spear farther than any man alive. His spirit always shined in his bright green eyes and strong smile, framed by the forest of brown curls about his head.

Skuli lifted his tunic on his left side, where a long clear scar was forming.

"Skuli does not forget, Gundar."

In their last battle, he had saved Skuli's life.

"It heals well, Skuli," Gundar responded.

"He would have finished me," Skuli said.

Gundar took the cup from Skuli and drank.

Skuli added, "Now maybe one day you will be needing Skuli's spear."

Gundar smiled, glad they were both alive, and tossed a few drops of water at him. "Until then, Valhalla can wait!"

Skuli smiled back. "Valhalla can wait."

The drum began again, and the men laid again into their oars. The sun was setting in their wake, a fiery orange globe streaking the bellies of the clouds.

On the open deck, the autumn wind was growing colder. He knew these seasons well, as he did this coast.

"Seven days and home!" Gundar yelled to all.

"Seven days!" a few answered in unison, their strength renewed.

"Thank Odin," Skuli yelled out, as the men leaned into their oars.

Gundar thought about their homecoming. In their long absence, many families would have endured great hardship. For some, greater hardship was still ahead. On that shore, fathers and mothers would mourn sons, and wives would wail over husbands lost. Then boys would be called to become men, and young girls, strong women.

So it was a bright seaside morning when they pulled their ship onto the hard-pounded gravel of the shore, and their families swarmed around. He did not look for Helga. She would never come down to ship or shore. Gundar had agreed. When that day came, if he did not return, she would bear her grief, alone, in the home they had built together.

Skuli broke his reverie. "Farewell, Gundar. You will see me again."

"No fighting without me, eh?" Gundar said kindly, picking up the pouch holding the scrolls.

"Don't make me wait too long," Skuli remarked.

They clasped their forearms and separated.

Gundar leaped over the gunwale onto the wave-splashed shore. He began walking across the wet tidelands, as the people hailed him, acclaimed by all as the great warrior he had become. His reputation had traveled back across the seas to his homeland in those years of his voyaging and his raiding. He nodded in acknowledgement as he passed through them, mindful that some would soon find their loves ones lost, as he headed toward a trail up the steep bluff.

Now as he climbed the winding trail along the cliff toward his home above, he watched far below on that rocky shore as each family found a son, a father, a husband, or went without. The sound of wailing and sorrow begins to rise from below, but the wind and surf soon drowned it out.

For himself, he was alive. Today the sun was bright on his face and the wind clear through his hair. Today no shadows would find him. He was home.

As he climbed over the top of the bluff, he removed his sweord belts, taking them into his hand with the two fine sweords his father had given him from the great metal smiths of the northern lands, and laid them down on the ground. This, too, he had agreed with Helga, not to bring war into their home.

When he looked up, they were there waiting – Helga, his wife, Thor, his nine-year-old son, eating an apple, and Lina, his beautiful six-year-old daughter. His stone house was there, as he remembered it, on the brown grassy hill below the snow-covered peaks towering behind. The apple trees he had planted were heavy with red fruit.

He laid his pouch down on the ground, as Thor ran to him, and jumped into his arms. He had grown so big he knocked Gundar back a step.

"Whoa! What mighty warrior is this?!" Gundar exclaimed, happy to see Thor's long straight blonde hair had grown down to his shoulders.

"Thor!" Thor answered proudly.

But Lina stood back by her mother, who watched and listened. He seemed a stranger to them now, he knew, after almost four years, in this place that was his home high above the cold winds of the North Sea. Here he had fathered them with Helga, and planted the apple trees that now stood over them.

He looked at Helga, who stood her ground and watched, not yet smiling. He waited, without calling to her, turning his attention back to Thor. He squatted, placing Thor down next to him and tousling his hair.

"Big as a mountain!" Gundar teased.

Thor punched him in the arm. "Bigger!"

Gundar reached out his arms to his daughter. "Lina." Her light brown curls fell in ringlets down to her shoulders, and her green eyes seemed wise beyond their years.

She came halfway to him. "Three winters!" she proclaimed, startling him.

Gundar, still holding Thor, kneeled down to her. "And now I am back."

"Are you sure?" she persisted.

"Yes, little Lina, I am sure," he answered softly.

Slowly, she, too, walked into his arms.

He looked up to Helga. For a moment, time was frozen as each held the other in the timeless gaze of that world that was theirs alone. Gundar opened his arm for her to join their embrace. She walked slowly toward him, tears in her eyes, finally remembering the man she had married.

He looked to Helga, repeating his words to his daughter, "I am sure."

He stood, and Helga walked into his arms, as though it was the first time she ever had. Their embrace was under the strong sun and the blue sky and the white billowing clouds. For him, it was the only embrace on earth. He had made it home.

They kissed, as Thor and Lina watched. They looked into one another's eyes, and Helga knew why she had waited, and Gundar, why he had returned.

Helga looked up to him, touching the scars on his arm. She looked at his hands, turning them over, seeing that they were whole and good. She smiled and looked into his face, into his clear blue eyes, and ran her fingers through his long blonde hair over his shoulders.

The light in her eyes filled his heart. Her smile opened as her eyes took hold of him, joyous at his return. "I have dinner for you. Good venison I traded for," she said.

"And I am hungry for it, Helga," Gundar answered, picking up his pouch and handing it to Helga to carry.

Gundar picked up his leather pouch, and put his arm around Helga's waist.

Helga smiled, eyeing the pouch. Plunder?" she asked.

Gundar shook his head. "New Gods…"

"New Gods? Don't we have enough of the old?" she teased.

Gundar picked up Lina in one arm and Thor in the other as Helga wrapped her arm around Gundar's waist. They walked back toward the cottage with Thor and Lina as the sun was setting red over the North Sea.

They made dinner and ate, and laid the children down to bed under their fur robes.

That night they made love. Holding one another naked skin to skin beneath the furs, the *fyr* of their love warmed them against the night's mounting chill. Like their first night, her soft skin and gentle movement comforted him, and lay to rest the dark visions of battlefields in foreign lands.

Now, as he lay naked beside her, feeling the warmth of her body and the smell of her hair, and the rise and fall of her breasts against his chest, he knew good dreams would come easily. Through the open window, he watched an early October snow falling like crystal shards in the bright moonlight. In the morning, all would be quiet under the deepening blanket of white.

It was a time he had long waited for…

CHAPTER TWO

THE WAR OF THE MORNING

"Gundar, we need to get the apples." It was Helga. Her voice was the morning sun to him, and always the sweetest thing in his life.

Gundar started. He was alone in the bed, and already the sun was high above the horizon. She had let him sleep, knowing that he needed it.

"You were tired," she said kindly.

His eyes, it seemed, were opening for the first time. He sat up. There was stone, and mud, and smoke-blackened timbers, lit by the golden light of early morning. The wind and ships and raging seas were gone, for now.

"The tree is full." Her voice was true, content. "But the snow will come early this year."

Helga. She was stirring a steaming stew in the stone hearth as the flame licked the blackened walls. He could smell the rich aroma of the mint and rabbit cooking.

His gaze traveled across the stones of the cottage to the oilcloth-covered windows where yellow light glowed down upon a bear-hide covered bed – everything was where it should be, and yet somehow everything was wrong. The light was different. The shadows were not the same – but the tawny color of her arms in the firelight, the smooth pearl of her skin as the orange flames reflected on the strong flesh of her shoulders – this he remembered.

"The leaves are still turning in the meadow. The colors are bright. We can walk there today," she said. "It will be warmer after the sun comes up."

Outside, he could hear the bare branches scraping against the stone walls of the cottage in the wind.

Helga was singing softly to herself. How he loved the gentle river of her voice shining in the sunlight of her bright spirit. She was happy, and her happiness filled his heart.

So long, he had been waiting for this time now, waiting to share life, to love her and be loved by her, through all the seasons. Helga. It was her strength that had sustained him through lonely nights on the icy battlefields, waiting for the letting of blood at dawn, when fierce metal flew angry against the bones of men. He watched her now, the muscles in her neck and shoulders rippling in the light of the hearth's flames. She, who had known battle, who herself had fought – she alone knew how to love him. She was there, always, waiting for him to return from the months and years, long campaigns of war, so they could rejoice in another season, together, alive.

He looked to her and she smiled back. The wars were over, for now. He was sure he had fought enough for a lifetime. For months his long blonde hair had remained stained red and hard with blood. He did not want to remember...

He stood to embrace her, meeting her shining blue eyes. Her beauty filled his heart and mind with happiness. "I remember the meadow," he smiled with memories they shared, kissing her.

But over her shoulder, his eyes were darting around the cottage for the glint of metal – his sweord, and found it, Still, always, that instinct in his belly – why now?

16

Helga steeped back. "Is everything all right?"

Helga always knew.

"Nothing." He looked though the open window to see Thor and Lina playing by the stream. He saw his son's bright face framed by long flaxen hair, smiling with eyes as blue as the southern seas.

He thought of those first years with her. They had been the happiest of his life. He had shared every season, with Helga, Thor, and Lina, the bright exploding colors of fall, the warming heat of summer, the excitement of new growth in spring, the inner nourishing time of winter. He had watched his son grow to a strong fearless young boy. He would watch him become a young warrior, and his daughter, the most beautiful girl of the village.

"Gundar?" her question floated toward him like a caress through his reverie.

Then he heard it – through the window.

"Gundar?" she asked again.

What was it? That sound. He turned.

"Helga..." Gundar half answered, thinking the children were too far way.

She smiled, but was stopped by his expression. "What is it, Gundar?"

With a single swift movement, he whipped his sweord from its leather-bound wooden scabbard.

He was moving on instinct toward the cottage door. His heart and belly were churning. Again, he heard it, louder, the distant crashing of running footsteps, rushing toward Thor and Lina!

Twenty strides away, Thor, sitting on the frozen stream, was already standing up, stepping forward in front of his sister, shielding her.

17

Gundar burst outside, sweord in hand, slamming the oak door into the cottage wall. The footsteps rushed closer, harder, crashing from the forest.

The ice bright diamond day pierced his eyes, and he held up his hand to shield them, for an instant slowing him.

Helga rushed through the door behind him. "Gundar! Thor?! Lena?!"

Thor, his back to the cottage, was turning directly toward the racing, crashing footsteps. The flapping of heavy leather armor roared and clattered bursting through the thrashing brush.

Thor and Gundar saw the warrior explode from the trees and in that instant, both knew.

"Stand tall!" Gundar yelled. "Thor!" Stand like a warrior at the gates to Valhalla, Gundar thought, shouting, "Look at him!"

But his words were not needed. Already, Thor stood strong in all of his nine years, fearless, staring at the approaching warrior in absolute stillness, so still the light breeze lifted wisps of his hair from his head.

Gundar took the warrior's measure – six and a half feet tall, bearskin robe, leather breastplate, leggings and broadsweord, rushing toward Thor as four more warriors cleared the brush. They would take Lina, not kill her, he knew.

The first warrior was seven strides from his son.

"NOOOOOOOOOOOOOO!" Gundar's wail filled the sky as he rushed forward, matching the warrior pace for pace.

He reached Thor as the warrior plunged his sweord through Thor's belly, and then lifted his sweord to block Gundar's crashing blow from above. But as quickly as he moved, Gundar moved faster. With his other hand, Gundar whipped from his belt a long dagger, driving it under the chest bone of his attacker, and pivoting round with mighty force swinging his sweord to behead his enemy, and swinging down again in full fury, hacking a bloody river into the corpse even as it fell toward the ground...as though his anger might turn back time.

"Momma!" he heard Lina cry as another warrior carried her off into the brush.

Two more warriors leapt upon him. He swung his sweord circular sideways, the first striking and breaking through the metal helmet, and spinning in reverse, cleaved the second warrior nearly in half as two more warriors attacked him. Rushing forward, he rammed one warrior with his shoulder, knocking him senseless to the ground – his first sweord blow slashed the other warrior's neck. The blood spurted ten feet. Before the fallen warrior could get up, he ran his sweord through his chest, and then raced to his son.

Helga was running out from the hut, spear in one hand and bow in the other, shouting, racing toward them, calling, "Thor!"

Gundar, kneeling down, looked into Thor's eyes. "Do not die," he commanded. For a moment, the force of Gundar's will sustained the life in Thor, and his eyes opened wider as he shuddered, fighting to fill his father's command.

"Gundar!" Helga's cry pierced the air, just as six more warriors burst from the forest, causing Gundar to look up in rage, renewed in bloodlust, thankful for it.

A rush of wind brushed past his face – he snapped his gaze back to see the downward stroke of

Helga's spear throw, and then forward to see the spear shoot through a warrior, throwing him back dead into the brush. Then, without breaking stride as she raced to Thor, she lifted her bow to fire two arrows into the throats of two more warriors, dropping them instantly to the ground.

Helga reached Thor as Gundar went forth with a roar to meet the three onrushing warriors. She kneeled down to him, covering his bleeding stomach with both hands as the red blow flowed through her fingers.

Gundar whipped his axe from his belt, flying it into the chest of one attacker with such force he was thrown back through the air to the ground. He leaned his shoulder to hit another below the waist, letting him roll over his own back, running his sweord through his chest even before he hit the ground. The remaining warrior halted short, looked at him, and ran.

A last groan from the nearest fallen warrior caused him to turn. Gundar threw both hands down upon him and yanked him to his feet.

"The girl! Where do they take the girl?!" he roared.

The man coughed up blood as Gundar shook him.

"North. To Trollveggen," he sputtered.

Gundar shook him again, more violently, yelling, "Trollveggen?! Why?!"

The warrior laughed, coughing up blood, spitting, "To fly," half-gurgling, "to fly...'" as he died.

Gundar looked into the lifeless eyes for more before throwing the corpse to the ground.

In the forest, the stirring of leaves faded with the footsteps of the last retreating warriors until there was silence – only the silence of death all around, until he began to hear the sound of his own labored breathing.

He turned to look back at Helga kneeling over his bleeding son. "They will take Lina north. I will have to track them," he said.

He pulled Thor up into his arms, holding him securely against his shoulder. In the distance, there was loud shouting from twenty or more warriors, approaching from the seaside.

Gundar, holding Thor, began running toward the mountains, yelling to Helga, "The ridge!"

Helga nodded, and looking around for further danger, ran after Gundar into the stony hills.

CHAPTER THREE

GOTH, STEALER OF LIGHT

Two huge warriors stood guard at the door to the hut, standing like pillars, clutching heavy axes dull from *bloodweorc*. Two more warriors, Heggr and Joarr, waited their turn inside. The early morning air hung still as ice.

Einarn arrived running, exhausted.

"They are all dead!" he announced.

"Praise Odin," one of the warriors said.

"No, no," Einarn protested, "Let me through."

Joarr and Heggr stepped aside.

Near the back of the hut, the fur wall seemed to be moving. Even among the tall Norsemen, Goth was a giant, two feet taller than most men, with arms thicker than a man's leg, and a head as large as a bear's. He paced slowly back and forth, his voice rumbling to himself.

Einarn waited, knowing not to speak first. Even the flames of the torches seemed to stand motionless. Oiled skins covered the two openings of the mud hut, darkening the sunlight. A low sullen *fyr* burned in the back hearth.

Goth turned.

"Only the boy!?" he roared like a wounded animal, his deep voice filling the hut. "They tell me only the boy! And not a clean kill! Where are they?!"

"They fought like demons, the woman, too. We have the girl," Einarn said.

"The body, where's the boy's body?"

"I could not get it. I would be dead." Einarn stated a fact.

"You <u>will</u> be dead!" Goth threatened in disgust. He turned away from Einarn. "You have only made him stronger."

"Einarn protested, "He fought like a berserker.""

"You are nothing. He is everything!" Goth spun around roaring, smashing his forearm across Einarn's face, throwing him crashing backward to the ground. "The boy must die! His woman must die! He must have nothing!"

Einarn picked himself off the ground, wiping the blood off his mouth. "He will never tell you their secret!" he protested.

Goth scoffed. "The scrolls are mine! My father died for them. He will tell me. He will tell me when it no longer matters to him. The boy was half of him, the woman the other."

Einarn spoke, "We still have time to go back. If the boy is still alive, they cannot travel with him."

Goth thought for a moment, and then commanded, "Out!"

Einarn ran out.

"Heggr! Joarr!" came the yell from inside, in a long deep roar that seemed to shake the stone walls of the house itself.

Heggr and Joarr entered. Goth was speaking. At times, they thought he seemed to be speaking to them, at other times, with himself. Heggr and Joarr knew well not to interfere with Goth's dark thoughts, yet fearing his anger when he expected an answer and got none.

"Only a fool would think to destroy his enemy by killing him...let his spirit loose, free from mortal pain, sure to strike back from the darker realms," Goth intoned. "That must not happen. Must not. Are you listening?"

Heggr stole a sideways glance to Joarr. Joarr watched Goth.

26

"Far better to keep him close, weaken his spirit," Goth continued, then suddenly grew silent again.

Joarr knew when Goth was silent there was danger. He and Heggr watched him closely, wary of his movements.

Then Goth laughed. "Come, Heggr, come," Goth gestured, stepping forward before the window, his shadow covering Heggr like a cloud covering the sun.

Heggr hesitated before stepping forward into Goth's shadow.

"Your plan failed. Your men are weak." Goth laughed again, placing his arm around Heggr's neck and shoulders. "You could not kill a woman?"

"She fought," Heggr answered, "with bow, and Gundar –"

"She fought!? Twelve men I gave you. Eh?" Goth asked, not wanting an answer.

"Gundar..." Heggr said, as though that was answer enough.

"Gundar," Goth repeated the name as though all answers were within it.

Suddenly Goth put his enormous hand around the side of Heggr's face and slammed Heggr's head into his chest. He began pressing Heggr's head against his chest, harder and harder, as Heggr struggled to escape. With his other hand, Goth reached for a goblet and drank. As he pressed harder, blood began to run from Heggr's nose and ears, and then pour. Goth let go and Heggr dropped dead to the ground.

Goth looked at him, spitting out, "Gundar." Goth put down his goblet and turned to Joarr.

Now Joarr saw another warrior, Vakr, had entered the hut. Vakr moved to block the door.

"Joarr," Goth called, waving him over. Joarr looked to Vakr and saw there was no escape. He hesitated.

"Come." Goth stretched out his arm. "It was not *your* plan."

"Lord," Joarr ventured, stepping forward.

Suddenly another warrior burst into the hut. "Goth!"

Joarr was thankful for the intrusion.

Goth spun around like an angry bear. His forearm smashed into the intruder's chest, knocking him back against the wall and pinning him there.

"Speak!" Goth roared.

Atti looked down at the body of Heggr. "News," Atti offered, as though giving a password that might release him.

Goth grunted and stepped back, releasing Atti.

"Words!" he commanded.

Atti looked at him without fear, as though used to Goth's moods. "They fled with the boy, or his corpse."

"Fled? Gundar?" Goth roared with laughter, and then stopped. "Did you see the boy's corpse?"

Atti shook his head.

"How many of your men are dead?" Goth asked.

"Eight," Atti intoned.

"There will be more," Goth nodded.

"We will kill the woman," Atti added.

Goth laughed again. "He will find you and more will die."

Atti raised an eyebrow.

Goth repeated himself. "Many more."

Atti waited for Goth's orders. Goth began pacing.

28

"Remember, only his woman. Gundar is mine. I will kill anyone who strikes him a mortal blow. Gundar must live. For now." Goth glanced sideways to Atti. "He will anyway."

Atti said nothing.

"This time make sure the boy is dead. Do not let them burn his body. Understand? We will take the girl north, and when Gundar follows, he will meet the northern winter. Let him first fight that."

Goth thought for a moment. "Take twenty men. You will need them if he finds you first. Go!" Goth commanded, and then added, "Don't touch the girl!"

Atti disappeared through the hide flap hanging over the doorway.

Goth grunted and turned back to Joarr. He reached for his goblet, drank from it, and handed it to Joarr.

Joarr, gaining a glimpse of hope in his action, took it and drank, keeping his eyes on Goth.

"Take two score men," Goth said calmly.

Joarr could not believe his ears. He was glad just to be getting out of the hut alive.

"Do you hear me?" Goth roared.

Joarr nodded, "Yes. Yes."

"You will take two score men, and finish this. Take the boy's body. Kill his woman. Do not touch the girl. Do you understand?"

Joarr nodded but did not know what to say.

"He will come for her!" Goth roared again, and then, seeing Joarr's consternation, added, "Atti is a fool. His efforts amuse me and Gundar will grow tired killing his men."

Joarr waited for more.

29

"Go!" Goth commanded.

Joarr looked to the door to see if the door was clear.

Even Vakr was not sure of Goth's intent. He hesitated, then seeing no other movement from Goth, stood aside, and let Joarr leave.

Vakr steeped forward and looked down at Heggr's corpse, and then shot a questioning look to Goth, wondering on the two different fates of Heggr and Joarr.

Goth read Vakr's thoughts. "Joarr will not fail me again." Then he began laughing, laughing so long finally Vakr had to join him.

Then as quickly as Goth started laughing, he stopped.

"Get out!" he yelled at Vakr.

Vakr left.

Goth began pacing again. "Winter will find you, Gundar, and you'll feel the jaws of Fenrir," Goth spoke aloud, as though his words might reach Gundar through the night.

He walked to a wooden chest with brown iron hinges and withdrew a small stone box. He opened it, carefully laying the top down beside it. Inside there was a bright silver cross on a silver chain. He took it out and dropped the chain and cross into his open palm.

He held the cross before his face, staring at it, closing his fist around it as a single word crossed his lips, "Father..."

* * *

Gundar was running into the forest, holding Thor close, Helga following. He followed the trail up the side of the ridge, away from the sea, his breath burning in his lungs, branches whipping against his face. He ran with Thor's life in his arms, not feeling the pain.

"Gundar, stop!" Helga was calling after him, "Gundar!"

He kept running. She ran harder, catching him, grabbing his arm.

"Stop!" she pleaded.

He slowed to a strong stride, the rhythm of his thoughts. Thor was dying. The attackers were escaping with Lina. Helga was not safe.

"Put him down, Gundar." Her voice was calm, a gentle command.

He looked into her eyes and knew she was right. He laid Thor down on the trail, and then stood.

Thor moved slightly on the ground.

Helga looked to Gundar, and he met her gaze, looking for the light in her eyes, but she denied him, breaking her gaze away.

Thor cried out.

Gundar looked down at him and then back toward the cottage.

"No, Gundar," she pleaded.

"My bow!" he said.

But it was not only his bow that was on his mind. It was the scrolls.

Helga knew. "It is for the scrolls you go. It was for the scrolls they came," she said, cutting him with her words.

Gundar looked at her and felt her judgment. "They may heal him," he answered.

"Their power is dark," she countered, "They brought his killers."

Her words cut deep. He buried the pain. "Take him to the head of the northern trail. I will find you!"

Helga just stared at him, and then turned away, kneeling back down to lift Thor up.

Gundar hesitated, then pushed back the questions rising inside him, and raced for the hut. He knew the attackers, if they were not still there, would return soon.

* * *

When he reached his home, Gundar slammed open the door of his cottage and grabbed his leather pouch. He looked inside to be sure the four scrolls were in it. What Helga had said was true. He could not speak the marks. He did not know what knowledge lay within them, but if *he* felt their power, maybe that power could help Thor live.

He grabbcd another sweord, his bow and quiver, his battle-axe, and his chest armor of layered reindeer hide. He saw some dried meat and threw it into the pouch. He took one last look around the hut, knowing he would never see it again, knowing the life he hoped to have there was gone. He started to leave but saw a small wooden toy he had once made for Thor.

He put it in his pouch, he ran out the door and back toward the ridge, his will pumping in his blood and muscles, driving him on beyond his body's endurance.

CHAPTER FOUR

THE ENDING OF THOR

Gundar returned to the northern trail, his bow and quiver, and broadsweord slung across his back. He carried two shortsweords, some small leather armor pieces, and his leather pouch. Two miles down the trail, he found Helga kneeling over Thor.

Thor looked up in agony, his torso bathed in dark crimson blood. Blood was running from the corners of his mouth. He had no strength to speak, or cry out.

Helga lifted her eyes from Thor, and seeing Gundar carrying his pouch, stared hard into Gundar's eyes. Gundar turned away, kneeling down to withdraw the scrolls from the pouch and lay them in a circle around Thor.

"He is dying, Gundar," Helga said.

Gundar watched Thor, but said nothing.

"He *will* die," she pronounced.

"He will not die," Gundar lied to her, and to himself.

"He will die slowly." Helga's words rang of truth.

She pulled a knife from under her robe. He looked at the knife and then into her eyes, but her eyes would not admit him. She raised the knife over Thor's heart.

He grabbed her wrist in a steel clutch. "He is strong!"

Thor moaned.

"Gundar..." Her voice reached out to him, with strength, guiding him.

"No." He had no other words.

"Look at him." Her voice forced a whisper driven from her heart. Their eyes locked.

He did not release her wrist. "He's my son."

"No less mine," she said.

Thor cried out again, in a cry of pain more horrible than either had ever heard. Their gaze broke as they both turned to look down at him.

Helga ran her fingers gently along Thor's temple, as though touching him for the last time.

Gundar stood and looked to the heavens, and then to the mountain horizon. "In the mountains, there are the healers. We'll find them. I'll carry him." Any words would do now, anything to fill the terrible silence fast approaching them. He slowly released his hold on her wrist.

Helga turned her face fully to him, beseeching him with her eyes, "The knife, Gundar. Take it."

Gundar could only keep looking at Thor now, unable to move his hand to take the knife.

Helga, still kneeling beside Thor, repeated herself, her voice steady, strong, looking up to him, "Take the knife, Gundar."

Gundar heard her words, strong and sharp, but some other force coursed through his blood and muscles, stopping his hand from moving.

Now he could only hear his own breath, moving in and out his chest. What was he listening to? What was he waiting for?

Gundar shook his head almost imperceptibly, but she saw it, appealing, begging, "Gundar..."

At that, Gundar looked up to her. "I am his father." But his words were hollow. He knew it. Now even his hundred battles could not bring him the courage he needed.

Helga looked at him, saw he would not do it. He would not take the knife. She turned her gaze from the fate she saw now rapidly approaching her. As though in a trance, she tightened her grip on her knife and raised it overhead.

"I give you my bloodoath, Gundar," she said, the blood running out of her fingers, turning them white, "You will regret this." Her voice was now only a haunting whisper, her words washing over Gundar as the cold waves of the long fiords.

She said nothing more. Her silence washed over him, filling his ears like a curse.

She drove the knife into Thor's heart.

Thor gasped once, and then was silent.

And then all was silent, and time stood still, for many long minutes, until a single leaf fell from a high branch. Gundar and Helga both watched it, hearing its wandering descent through the still forest air.

In their ears that sound became a deafening roar, and through Gundar poured and rushed the roar of darkness and grief, and the roar of anger. He looked down at Helga, the bloody knife in her hands. He looked into her eyes, Thor's lifeless body beside her. Then everything vanished from his senses, all sight and sound, and it was all he could do to stand against the wind trying to pull him through the gates to the underworld.

Helga threw the knife down upon the scrolls.

Her tears fell down covering Thor's face in a wet shroud.

Gundar forced himself to remain standing   *Fyr* flared in his mind and belly, erasing all thought. Now life would be too long to live.

She did not turn to him, or look at him, but remained staring into another world, into a forest devoid of any life. "It is growing late," she intoned without expression.

Gundar stared at the bloody knife on the ground. The morning sun glinted on the red wet iron. He knew Helga, in her heart, had left him. He gathered up the scrolls into his pouch, put on his reindeer hide armor, took his sweords and battle axe and stood, staring into the glaring horizon.

"Wait here," he said, but Helga was not moving and did not hear him.

Neither did Gundar move.

* * *

The warriors of Goth, led by Joarr and Bjorn, swarmed over Gundar's cottage. Bjorn slammed open the wooden door, knocking it off its hinges. The warriors rushed in. They tore down the hide from the windows to let in the sunlight, tossed up the table and benches, threw open the wooden chests, and dragged all the bear hides outside onto the ground. They ripped through the remaining clothes, emptied every box, and looked in every shelf and crevice. There was nothing there. Bjorn did not expect otherwise. He went out of the cottage and announced to Joarr, "He has hidden them."

"Taken them. He has taken them." Joarr disagreed.

"He had no time," Bjorn countered.

"He came back," Joarr smirked.

"Then he cannot be far," said Bjorn.

"No, he is not far," Joarr said, putting his hand to his sweord and looking around.

Bjorn, too, surveyed the landscape. In the hills behind the hut, he saw a trail cutting across the side of the hill, making its way toward the ridge.

"There," Joarr said, pointing to the trail. Then he turned back toward the hut and gave an order to his men, "Burn it!"

They threw their torches onto the thatch roof and the cottage burst into flames.

Bjorn smiled to himself, glad they had found nothing. He was eager for a fight.

Joarr saw his expression and yelled, "Fool! Goth will kill us both, if Gundar does not first."

Bjorn smiled again. "Gundar will not escape us. He is one. We are many."

"We were many before," Joarr stated.

Bjorn saw Joarr's expression and commented, not wanting to offend Joarr, "Now he is tired. We will take him."

A warrior stepped up to them. "We cannot find the boy's body. There is no grave."

Joarr nodded. "He carries the boy. We'll reach him before night falls."

Then something caught Joarr's eye. Leaning against a tree was a sweord. He walked to it and picked it up. He ran his hand over its face. He felt its weight. It was a fine sweord, etched in scrolls across its face.

A warrior asked, "He leaves it?"

He looked into the forest as though he might see the answer. Then he turned and walked into the field where the dead warriors lay, a killing field of hacked corpses.

It was a fierce morning's *bloodweorc* - with a sweord greater than this. He swung the sweord in his hand, cutting a four-inch tree through so it toppled. But he knew, compared to what Gundar must have, this sweord was nothing.

"Take it," he said to one of the warriors. "For Goth. He will want something."

Joarr walked amongst his slain warriors, smiling to himself.

"Gundar's reputation in the southern raids is well deserved, as mine will be when I capture him," he said.

Bjorn overheard him "Ours," he corrected.

Joarr ignored his comment, looking to his men, who awaited his orders.

"Kill his woman. The boy is dead by now. Find his body and take the head," he said, looking again to the horizon, secretly relishing the chase ahead.

CHAPTER FIVE

THOR'S REVENGE

Gundar was running, weaving through the forest, loping like a wolf, barely feeling the sting of branches whipping across his face. Battle-lust burned in his blood, trampling thought and feeling with thundering instinct as he looked forward in rage so as not to look back in sorrow.

His lungs heaved and burned inside his chest as he pushed himself over hills and waded leaping through rushing icy creeks, not feeling the splash of water over his thighs. Then he stopped…and listened.

While his chest was heaving, he thought of the scrolls. He was glad he had hidden them amongst the roots of a rotted tree trunk.

Now, he waited. At first, there were only the forest sounds, the birds, the small animals, and the light breeze in the branches. He listened, holding his breath still, until at last he heard other sounds, distant and faint, human voices – his prey.

As the voices grew near, his muscles tensed, his chest rising and falling as his breath returned. He found himself staring through the filtered light at the tree branches covered in a clear coat of ice. He broke off a small branch, rubbed it between his thumb and forefingers. For a few seconds, it calmed him. He broke it in the middle, watching a glistening drop of sap form on the inner white pulp. Even after the leaves had fallen.

He peered into the forest. The mist was still rising from the ground into the trees as the sun cleared the distant hill, piercing the white mist with virgin yellow rays. Now this hunt was all he knew, all he could do. He had to keep moving. Always keep moving.

Now memories overtook him...he was thirteen...in the clash and rain of blood-sprayed battle, his father, Avangar, stood alone, his hearth-companions falling all around him. The enemy warriors were massing around him like wolves, their bearskin robes flying with each sweordstroke, hiding him from view. "Father!" Gundar called out and swung pivoting a two-armed blow, driving his sweord across his attacker's belly. He fell, the last of three Gundar had defeated. Gundar could see the battle had moved on, toward his father's stance – there where the enemy thronged thickest. He froze, uncertain.

Suddenly, from the forest, another enemy horde rushed, brandishing spears, shouting terrible animal cries.

Avangar heard them. "Run, Gundar, run!"

And then he ran, to obey his father, or because he was afraid to die. He did not know. He would never know. He ran, even as he heard his father's last cries as the warriors slew him with a hundred blows.

...the sound of voices on the stream brought him back. They were drawing closer. How many? Between him and his daughter? On the northern trail there would be more. And almost four hundred miles to go.

First, he must break the trail by those who had found him. Then thirty miles per day. Thirteen days. Thirteen days to live or die, for Lina to live or die. When he got there, would she be alive? When he returned, would Helga be?

Gundar tested the ice with his weight – it would hold. He slipped through the thicker brush by the stream's edge, making his way downstream. He could hear them now, speaking loudly and without fear,

44

emboldened by their own number. He listened, counted their number with each new voice he heard. He did not care how many. They could meet his axe with the false courage of the herd. He followed the trail down the stream, moving carefully to avoid making any sound. At last he was close enough, and their voices were as loud as though he were in their midst.

Coming to a clear patch of ground, gathering his will and force, he rushed forward with all his speed, and leapt onto the stream's smooth ice, sliding downstream like a spear. He balanced his weight and pulled his axe from his belt. The warriors looked up, too late.

With a great roar, Gundar swung his axe full circle overhead, crashing it down through the helmet of Joarr, so his lower jaw fell onto the ice. With his other hand, he ran his sweord across the throat of another warrior, and still sliding, hacked through the breastplate of a third, killing him instantly. Spinning round he swung his axe to slice off the leg of another warrior. Four more warriors came running to the stream, but Gundar was already disappearing into the trees, vanishing as a deadly ghost.

Gundar circled back to their encampment. He let fly his axe, cleaving the face of the sole guard. He ran to pull his axe and push it back into his belt. He took two spears leaning against a tree and ran back to the stream. When he spotted them again, he hurled the two spears with lightning speed one after another. Both found their mark in the chests of two warriors. Then with a roar, he rushed the other three warriors. One let fly a spear as they rushed toward one another. Gundar spun, catching the spear, and turning in full circle took its motion round to throw it back into the face of his attacker, even as another spear sliced his upper arm.

Enraged, Gundar threw his sweord through the warrior's chest, and pulled his axe from his belt.

Bjorn leapt toward him with axe and another warrior with sweord. He dodged the axe blow, and blocked the sweord blow with the haft of his axe, swinging his elbow in the warrior's face so hard it snapped his neck. He traded blows with Bjorn, axe against sweord, until with a great blow, he cleaved Bjorn's helmet through, so the blood spurt from his eyes.

The shouts of dying men filled the forest.

Gundar moved faster than their dying cries, striking down a warrior at their eastern perimeter, and then moving fast and silent as a wraith to the northern perimeter to strike down another. A few fast strides into the center, and he let fly his axe forty yards to the southern perimeter and another fell.

One by one, the voices fell silent, until only the fleeing steps of a single warrior remained.

Gundar pulled his axe from the chest of a dead warrior, and then, with a wail, swung it deep into the nearest tree. With none now left to kill, he let himself fall leaning into a tree. His chest was heaving, and his breath roaring. Now it was the silence he wanted to kill, the silence that filled him and possessed him and rang inside him like a great bell over a still sea.

Gundar wailed to fill the silence, and when his breath gave out, he spoke from his heart.

"I cannot bring you back. I cannot bring you back, Thor."

But the silence gave no answer.

All was quiet in the seaside village on the shores of southwest Greenland. It was the kind of deep quiet that was waiting to be broken by something out of the ordinary.

As Bjarni Herjolfsson slept with his wife Berta, tossing and turning for reasons he did not know, they were disturbed by a loud knock at the door.

Bjarni growled, "Go away."

The knocking continued, louder. Bjarni growled again, "Get out!"

"Bjarni, Bjarni!" the panicked voice yelled.

Berta threw off her covers and put on a robe. "It's Tueggi! I will see what it is."

She returned shortly with a shocked look on her face. "Your ship, Bjarni! It sails!"

"What?! It cannot sail!" Bjarni exclaimed.

Bjarni jumped out of at bed in his nightshirt and ran through the door.

When he made it to the shore his ship was already two hundred feet onto the water, its oars carrying it away, its bright red striped sail unfurling. He peered through the night unable to see the thieves, but his answer came in the form of a booming voice.

"I buy your boat, Bjarni!" he heard from across the water.

Bjarni yelled back, knowing the voice instantly, "Leifr Eiriksson, you son of a whore, bring my boat back!"

"And I will, soon enough, filled with wine and women, and gold from the new land!"

"No, no, no, you'll be roaming the sea forever, you idiot! It was only a saga!" Bjarni protested.

"As mine will be. Good-bye, Bjarni," Leifr yelled, waving a farewell as the ship disappeared into the wide bay.

"Eiriksson!" Bjarni yelled.

Suddenly he felt a slap to the back of his head. "Women?!" Berta complained. "Where do you think he got that?!"

"*Mange takk*, Bjarne!" was the last voice he heard from the ship as it vanished into the dim light of dawn.

* * *

Helga had not moved from her spot beside Thor's body when Gundar arrived.

She looked at him, covered with blood, some running down his leg.

"You are wounded," she said.

Gundar shook his head. "There will be fewer on the trail now." He gathered up his scrolls on the ground and placed them in his pouch.

He picked up Thor's body and put him over his shoulder, looking up the hill.

"Up there was a hut," he said.

"Still..." she confirmed, nodding.

He walked up the ridge. "They will not attack at night."

* * *

At dawn, sounds stirred him, branches breaking. Fast footsteps circled the hut where they had slept. He jumped up.

"Helga!" he whispered.

Helga was already awake, sitting against the wall of the hut holding out his arrows.

Gundar, bow in hand, surveyed the hut. The longbow he had fashioned and learned to draw as a boy was taller than a man, and held twice the power of an ordinary bow. It could pierce a leather breastplate or even chain mail at close range.

Gundar peered out the window, but no warriors were visible. The invaders were wise to be cautious – Gundar's reputation with the bow was known and feared.

He observed the windows in the hut, one in the front, two on each side. He counted his arrows – only ten. How many were out there? He glanced at Helga. Eighteen or twenty, he thought. His eyes met Helga's. He pointed in a circular motion, stopping to point at each window. He held up two fingers. Two arrows at each window.

He had calculated the distance to the forest, about forty yards.

They would come all at once across the clearing, testing him at first, and then sending more. The back of the hut, against the high cliff, he knew would be unassailable.

49

He would need a second for each shot, a second to move. If he missed, when he moved to the next window there would be a warrior leaping through the window to his side. He looked at Helga. There was no fear in her eyes, but she saw what he saw. He could not miss, if they were to survive.

"You will not miss," she said.

He said simply, "They will come now."

She nodded. They had both been in battle. It was not a time for words. He took an arrow from her outstretched hands and notched his bow.

He stood at the center window.

The first wave came, three in the center, two on each side, the warriors shouting wildly as they rushed in.

His first arrow shot through a heart, knocking one back, his next, a throat. With no time to watch them fall, he moved to the next window. Helga stood beside him, holding arrows out for his swift grab. Again, his arrow flew through a chest, and another. Four were down. At the third window, the two racing warriors, now closer, were easy targets. Their leather breastplates were of no use. Six were dead. Pivoting around, and stepping back to the center window, the seventh warrior, almost at arms length, saw his own death in Gundar's eyes as he faced Gundar's bow, and then was gone.

But the last shot had broken Gundar's bowstring, and more were coming. "It's broken," he said, looking at Helga's long hair that fell to her waist, realizing it could be braided into the bowstring he needed.

He commanded her, "Your hair!"

Helga looked at him without moving. An arrow flew into the hut, striking through a wooden strut.

"Your hair!" he yelled. "Helga! My bow!"

Helga looked at him, fierce in her will, doing nothing. "Now remember my bloodoath, when I took my knife to my son's heart."

"Then your bloodoath will kill us both," he said.

"You are the man. Do what you will," Helga answered.

Gundar, too proud to ask again, said only, "So you have kept your bloodoath." Another arrow flew into the hut, brushing Gundar's arm so that it began to bleed.

"Now think of our daughter, who is all that remains," Gundar spoke.

Mention of their daughter fractured Helga's defiance. "All that remains...." She turned her back to him, so he could cut her long strands for his bow.

He pulled his knife, holding her hair fast in his fist, to cut the long strands. In seconds, he had fashioned them into a bowstring and re-strung his bow. He looked at the three remaining arrows. Each one would have to count.

But the warriors were more cautious now, standing back in the trees. He drew the bow to its full extension. The warrior was behind a tree a hundred yards away. As the warrior stepped around it, Gundar fired. The sound of the arrow's flying death was the last thing that warrior heard as it shot him through the throat.

The remaining warriors saw him collapse gurgling in blood and spoke to each other with their backs pressed against the trunks of huge trees.

"We need more men," one said.

"You want to tell Goth that we failed?" the other asked.

"You can die here. I'll take my chances with Goth," the first answered.

They remaining warriors all nodded and slipped back into the forest.

* * *

"Are they dead?" Helga asked.

"Dead or gone now," Gundar answered, watching through the window.

They both looked at Thor.

"I will bury him," Gundar said.

"No!" Helga said.

He had never heard her speak in that tone before, and he knew her decision was absolute.

"I will give him the *fyr*," she said.

"The *fyr* –" he said.

"– will bring them," she answered.

"They'll kill us," Gundar stated.

"Kill *me*, if they can," she said flatly.

He looked at her. Now there was another kind of silence between them.

He offered her a shortsword. She took it without answering him.

"Helga," he said, "build it high, and run."

"Find my daughter," she replied. "I will not die today."

He wanted to know her heart, but said nothing, asked nothing of her.

Gundar looked at her and took one of two silver serpent bracelets off his arm and placed it on hers. "My ring-oath I will bring her to you."

She took it from him, watching as he pulled the scrolls from his pouch, unrolled them and folded them flat.

"Go inland to Skyrnsgard," he said. "They will not follow you there." He pulled a long piece of sinew from a pocket. He folded the scrolls into flat sheets and tied them across his stomach under his tunic. "They will not kill her. It is not their plan." Gundar did not know what was true, but he knew he wanted Helga to be safe.

Helga looked at him, but said nothing.

Gundar walked a few steps up the hill. Helga saw his dark silhouette against the red glow of sunset.

Then he turned to depart, and ordered, "Stay alive, Helga."

Helga saw the fierce grip on his sweord, turning his knuckles white, and the tension running through his whole body, now locked, rigid, ready.

"Kill them all," Helga said, and turned to lift up Thor's body.

Gundar watched Helga move silently and swiftly away with the body of Thor over her shoulder, in a stride driven by anger and grief.

She marched for three hours without stopping or even breaking stride. She knew she would need time and distance between her and her attackers if Thor were to have a sacred burial by *fyr*.

When she reached the tree line, she laid his bloody body in the cradle of roots of a giant tree. She caressed his hair away from his face. He was a handsome boy – he would have been a more handsome man. He was at peace now. His spirit, too, would soon be at peace.

She looked around, spotted a stand of small straight aspen trees. They would do. She took her shortsweord from her belt and approached the first tree. She put her hand around it to test its girth. Then she bit into the bark with her first stroke. Then another, and another.

She tried to focus on her *weorc*, but as much as she tried, she could not keep Gundar from her mind. He would come and she would push him out. She tried not to think about him, to not feel him. She needed her strength.

The last tree was nearly cleaved through. With another hard blow, her shortsweord broke. She shook the tree in a tight grip above the cut and it broke. She let it fall to the ground. She began again, thinking of the wood, the *fyr*, not wanting to think of Gundar. She felled another tree and another. She made another blow, but her sweord shattered, worn from the *weorc*. She cut the last two with her knife, hacking and slicing through the wood. Finally, there were enough. She gathered them up and dragged them to a high mound. She built her alter, a square cross-piling of timber. She laid six trees across the top to form a platform eight feet above the ground. Working feverishly, she piled brush and sticks against the wooden structure.

She looked over to the horizon. The sun was growing red as it dipped toward the far hills. So be it then. The *fyr* would glow like a beacon at night. Let them come, they who had taken her son, they who did not fear a woman's wrath.

She lifted Thor's body up and placed it on the altar. She laid the broken shortsweord by his side, carefully putting the two pieces together to make it whole.

"Go safely to Valhalla, my son, and I will join you soon enough."

With flint and sweord, she struck sparks to light an ember into a piece of charred cloth, and then blew it into flame. Carefully she lighted the dry brush and grass. The flames caught. As she watched them grow on that cold hillside, to flames ten feet high, they grew also within her, consuming her last denial of Thor's death.

They would come now. She would have to fight. But she would not put her son in the ground. Not now. Not ever.

The tall flames licked up the logs toward the darkening sky. When they reached Thor's body, she turned her head. Then she looked up at the surrounding ridges. She would have to wait to defend the sacred *fyr* until it had done its *weorc* of carrying the Thor's spirit to Valhalla. Then she would run into the forest, into the night.

It was then that she saw them, two warriors running down the trail from the ridge top. They would reach her in minutes. Instinctively, she put her hand to her belt. She looked back to the *fyr*. Not yet. Not yet. She studied the ground, looked for the high point. She surveyed the forest for the trail. It opened into a wide grassy area. No chance for surprise. She would take the high ground, without a sweord, only her long knife. She would need something more. She could hear their running now.

She ran to the *fyr* and pulled a burning log from the pile. With her knife, she began sharpening the end into a sharp point. It was too heavy to use as a throwing spear. She returned to the mound and put the pointed log at her feet. The second warrior she would have to fight knife against sweord. They were crashing though the underbrush now, sliding and running down the shale slope.

"Odin, give me strength," she prayed. Then she picked up the log. The warriors emerged from the trees. Helga yelled and rushed into the first warrior, plunging the killing log through his body. Then she leaped to one side, escaping the sweord stroke of the other. He swung again and she blocked it with her knife. He drove her back, stroke after stroke. It was only a matter of time. Then she remembered something Gundar had told her. In the last breath, there is victory. Where was it now? The warrior's stroke slid down her knife to the hilt. He smashed his forearm into her face and she fell back, still standing. Helga leaped for the slain warrior's sweord, rolling across the ground to pick it up.

The warrior laughed, "You make it a good fight!" But as he laughed, she had already tossed her sweord into the air, letting it fall back into her hand like a spear.

"I speak for my son." She launched it with a ferocious throw that shot through his mouth emerging through the back of his head.

"I speak for Thor," she pronounced, as he collapsed to the ground.

She was breathing so hard her throat seemed aflame. More warriors were racing down the trail. She looked back to the *fyr* and saw Thor's body burning. A

56

tear ran from her eye. She pulled the sweord from the dead warrior, and picked up his. Being too heavy to carry, she broke both of them on a rock, and turned to see four more warriors running up the hill. She glanced at Thor's burning body. In three minutes, at the most four, he would be gone. She could defend his spirit to the very end, or run into the forest. She was not afraid to die, but at that moment, she thought of Gundar, and knew she wanted to see him again. She glanced again at the men, at Thor's body, and the forest's edge.

"Thor..." With his name, she gave Thor's body to the flames and to the gods. She turned toward the trees and ran, skirting the tree line, so they would pursue her, and allow a longer time for Thor's passage to Valhalla. In her anger, she wanted to stay and fight, but she would not die today. With a last look toward Thor, she slipped into the forest.

The trees were thick and night was approaching. Soon she no longer heard the running footsteps of her pursuers behind her. She slowed her pace to a walk as the moonlight began to drape the branches' skyward edges with silver and cover the forest floor with a black lace of shadows.

She thought of her daughter, and Gundar.

CHAPTER SIX

THE MARCH OF THE HUNTERS

Only a hundred yards from the rocky coast, Goth's great warship rode the frothing waves, boasting sixty war shields hung on each side. At its bow, a fierce carved dragon twenty feet high ruled the seas ahead.

Goth stood on the bow, a hand on the figurehead to steady himself. He watched the shoreline pass a hundred yards away and the white billowing clouds float above. He looked back to see Lina sitting on the bench near the rear of the boat. He was thinking of Gundar.

One of his warriors approached him.

"The traders from Dubh Linn will be waiting." Blokr said,

Goth did not seem to hear him. He was still thinking of Gundar.

"Lord?" Blokr asked.

"Wheat, wool, and tin, and tin and wheat and wool," Goth said. "The dogs want my gold. Twice the price than if I sailed there myself."

Blokr warned, "If they trade to the south, without us, we will have no food for the winter."

"The grass grows through the snow," Goth said, and added, "If Thorgils can conquer a kingdom with ten thousand men, why cannot I destroy one man with a hundred?"

Goth turned to the other warrior.

"Where is he now?" he asked.

"He heads toward the village of no hands," the warrior answered.

"Yes, the *weorc* of our good king...let him see....Has the girl been eating?!" Goth asked.

The man looked at him, "I did not know..."

Goth pushed him aside and strode back past the men rowing in unison as they beat their oar blades.

He approached Lina and spoke.

"Tell me your name," Goth said.

Lina glared up at him and said nothing. Goth was surprised, but respected her fearlessness. He took a long deep breath as he considered what he wanted from her.

"I am Goth," he said. He sat down so as not to tower over her, and then, seeing he still did, sat on the deck to be even lower.

"Goth," he repeated quietly.

Lina said nothing.

"Lina...your father..." Goth paused, wanting to speak true.

Still she said nothing.

"My father was a chieftain...your father killed him. That is why I took you." He was not sure why he wanted her to know, or understand.

At that, Lina looked up. "Killing is bad." Then she added, "Is that why you killed my brother?"

Goth grunted. She had agreed with him while condemning him.

How did she know? Yet she knew.

"It was his fate," Goth sad, denying his involvement to himself.

"You did it, didn't you?" Lina said.

He looked at the young child, with her arms wrapped around herself, and saw that she was cold.

He smacked Vigmar on the back of the shoulder. "Don't your eyes see?! Give her your coat!"

"I don't want it," Lina said. She looked at him, and added, "My father is strong, you know. Stronger than you."

Goth stood, meeting her eyes, and then left, shouting to his men and to the wind, "Row, row like the jaws of Fenrir are at your back! Row, you weaklings! Row!"

* * *

Helga had been running for more than an hour. The light in the forest had grown less, the forest sounds, more. The moonshadows were growing long and intermingling on the needle-covered forest floor, as night took hold. She slowed her pace to a fast walk. Finally, her breath became more even.

As her pace slowed, and her thoughts came home to her, she realized that for the first time since Thor was born she was alone. She was falling, falling through stone. It was an aloneness she would not accept, an aloneness she had to stop.

What was she doing, she thought. The trails were only leading deeper into the forest, to unknown villages where she knew no one. Gundar wanted her to go inland, but the more she thought about it, the more she realized she would be isolated. Safe, but isolated. She would be able to contribute nothing to the search for their daughter.

They had tried to kill her, and failed. They were hunting her but by now must have lost her trail. She slowed to a stroll, and then finally stopped. She knew she wanted to go back.

She looked back toward the coast, considering what she might do. Who would help her now? Whom did she know? Whom could she trust? She could think of only one man, the man Gundar had told her about. Skuli. She knew his village. She could be back there in one or two days. She knew a seldom-traveled trail to the outskirts of the village. No one would be watching it.

It was a risk, but Gundar would need help if she were ever to see her daughter again. She had not let herself feel anything for Gundar all this time, or even hope for his safe return. She could not let her heart go there. Her pain would not let her. Her own anger she did not even know yet.

She turned and began walking back toward the western horizon, and the setting red sun. She felt a renewed strength in her stride. There was no time to waste.

*   *   *

Gundar had begun his trek north through the coastal mountains and forests. He realized the ways of the land were not familiar to him. It was not the sea, and he would have to learn how to cross it while he traveled it.

With each step, he knew he was leaving Helga behind, and wondered if he would ever see her again.

A wolf howled, and then another. Small animals were moving in the underbrush now. They were safer in the night than he – they had lived and moved in it longer. Somehow, he would have to learn their ways, to move with them. All his life he had been taught to rarely move at night, and then only when he knew the path was clear. Now he was walking beyond dusk into the darkness, and sometimes through the night.

He was alone now without any scouts to report the terrain or enemy ahead. He would have to strike when they expected him to hide, to hide when they expected him to strike. Maybe he would retreat when they attacked, attack when they were retreating. His every movement and decision would mean his life now, his daughter's life, Helga's life.

After several hours, he stopped to rest, leaning into the roots of a giant tree, and pulling his fur garments over himself.

He awoke even before the first signs of light. He felt the dawn moving his blood. He shook the cold from his bones and the angry dreams from his heart, and set out on the northern trail again. He began to see signs of their passing, his son's killers. He was realizing they had made no effort to hide their trail after them. Everywhere branches were cut or broken, stones rolled aside to make their path. So they did not fear him, he thought. They even expected him to follow them. They were leading him on when they could have far outpaced him. Why? He had no answer and no choice but to follow.

He descended the trails down the coastal cliffs toward a small village that sat on the low cliffs above the sea. It was a village he had often seen from the water as they sailed past, but had never visited. Now, growing closer, he heard the ringing of bells. He had often heard them in the monasteries on the distant coasts, but not here.

The new religion had brought it. Its priests wanted it. While most of the people still believed the bells drove away the nature spirits, the priests believed it brought purification. He wondered what the scrolls might say.

As he approached the outskirts of the village, he saw no one working in the fields. Horses and cows were untended or stood ignored in their sheds. The usual sounds of village life, the women laughing as they worked, the ringing of the smith's hammer and anvil, the barking of the half-wild dogs, were absent. No carts were on the village paths. No people were walking. Even the clouds above it seemed hung too low and still.

He thought to draw his sweord but something in him told him to wait. No one and nothing approached him. The air was so still he could feel it parting before him as he walked.

As he entered the rows of stone cottages, wide-eyed women and unkempt children stood in the doorways and looked out from around the edges of windows, not wanting to be seen.

No one spoke to him or looked at him as he walked through the village. A strange and heavy silence filled the paths and fields. No children were playing. No craftsmen were working. There was no sound in the dead air except for the church bell ringing.

Then he began to see them. They sat on benches around the village square, or on the ground, leaning against the stone well. Blind men with empty eye sockets, men with no hands, some with no feet, sat on the ground and lay about the square on wooden benches. A few spoke to one another. Most waited, for nothing. Some stared into space. The blind and crippled were everywhere, as many as those not afflicted.

A few men looked up when he entered the square. Most did not. He watched, by the open well, an old man trying to dip a cup into the water by holding it between the stumps that were his wrists, swinging them into the leaf-strewn pool of water.

Gundar approached him to ask, "What plague came here?"

"You can see it!" the old man answered, going back to his efforts.

"I asked you, what plague?" Gundar demanded.

"Plague? No plague. Plague…Olaf is the plague, with his new god," the old man answered. "By the order of the king they said. What king?!"

"Who is this Olaf that he would do this?" Gundar asked.

The old man looked around before speaking, shaking his head sadly.

"They came at night, bringing the new religion. Many here wanted to stay with the old ways. Some were banished, the ones that remained….he cut off their hands or feet. Some they hanged or cut their heads off, if they were too much trouble," the old man said. "Is that the new gods? Is this the new world they want?"

Gundar took the cup and dipped it into the well, holding it up to the old man's mouth to drink. He took his fill as Gundar looked around, finally hearing the sound of weeping coming through the windows of one of the huts.

The old man offered him a piece of bread and then water from his cup, between the stumps of his wrists. Gundar shook his head, unable to accept any kindness from any so troubled.

"A man, not a god, did this, "Gundar said.

The old man held up his bandaged hands. "Man or god? God or man? I have no hands! I have no hands, Gundar."

Gundar stepped back. "You know me?! You know my name?"

"Words echo in these hills," he said, "They will enslave your daughter for their whims, if she lives."

"You have seen her?" Gundar asked.

"No, she was not with them," the old man answered.

"How do I reach Trollveggen?" Gundar asked.

"Trollveggen? You cannot. It's hundreds of miles, north of Raumalen. You can only go by sea. Unless you cross the valley of the ice lakes, but that no one has survived," the old man explained. "But why go to the cliffs of Trollveggen?

"Cliffs?" Gundar asked.

"Higher than a hundred masts," he nodded.

Gundar stood, remembering the words of the warrior at his hut, 'to fly, to fly…' "Then I have little time." He turned to leave but then stopped. "I will kill this king if I see him. I will kill any of his men I find."

Suddenly two warriors with sweords drawn stepped out from behind a stone wall.

"Start here, traitor!" the first challenged.

Gundar drew his sweord as a third warrior watched from afar.

"Stand back or die!" Gundar answered.

The warriors laughed, not knowing who they were facing, and lunged at him.

Gundar leapt between them, spinning to slash their sides, killing them with four lightning strokes. The third warrior fired an arrow through his hide breastplate, but the shaft broke, leaving only the head in his armor, missing his flesh. Then the warrior fled.

"Go," the old man yelled. "They'll come now. All of them. More! This door you cannot close! Go! They will be ahead of you and behind. Every trail!"

Gundar nodded, and rushed out of the village center. He passed the burned ruins of a church, the dragon's head that once adorned it lying charred on the ground. Nearby, a priest in colored robes made an up and down and back and forth motion with three fingers over the bowed head of a blind man.

He had seen it before. It was called the sign of the cross – the Father, the Son, and the Holy Spirit. Heaven and earth, and what bound them together, the priests said. He wondered how it could be bound, what to him now seemed forever torn apart.

He continued walking. Everywhere here, there was sorrow and destruction, and boundless death beyond lamenting. This village was lost for a generation. The chain of life had been broken. The rule of the gods had been shattered here. He would not ask for food here. Not ask for anything.

He put his hand around the edge of his leather pouch and walked out of the village, toward the forest above the coastline. He grabbed the shaft of the broken arrow in his chest armor, and pulled it out, tossing it to the ground. He knew, in killing this new king's men, he had opened a door he could not close, but he put the thought from his mind and marched on.

From the far distance, the ocean winds rose over the great seaside cliffs and blew into the mountain valley, carrying him on. He wanted to put the village from his mind, as though the violence wrought upon those wretched might run red into the clear water of hope he held onto in the scrolls. This could not be their teachings, he thought. He would not let it be their teachings. He walked hard, trying to hold to his belief in them, and his hope that they might somehow help him.

Soon the path wound back toward the coast to end at a cliff wall towering above the sea. The mountains here reached down to the North Sea, meeting the shore with great cliffs thousands of feet high. To the north, he knew no roads or paths crossed the land for two hundred miles. That was the forbidden land, the land of the ice lakes, inhabited by all things that opposed man, and his purposes. To reach it, he would have to first go west.

Gundar walked to the land's edge and looked down to the ocean waves far below. They would round the peninsula and take Lina north along the coast. The winds were not blowing strong. Still, they would sail with her, hoping the winds would return as they pulled on their oars. The seas were heavy now, and the wind light. They would make their way slowly.

He considered his course. He, too, could build a boat, but he might lose more time. They might find him as he worked. They would row with fifty or sixty men. He would have a single sail. If the winds did not come, all would be lost. The path over land, west and north across the peninsula, was filled with danger, but he could face it, and make his way by his will.

His mind was running. He knew his mind was running. No plan could come now. He drew a deep breath, and then another. He forced himself into his senses. He looked at the tree branches, watching them and listening as they brushed one against another. He slowed his breath, breathed as the wind in those branches, until his thoughts had quieted. Here he would make camp, hopefully to awaken in the morning with a clear mind and purpose.

He looked for a place to pass the night. Above him on the slope was an opening amongst the trees that led to a cliff face above. It would serve as a rear defense. He walked to the cliff base, throwing down his broadsweord. He began to gather firewood. Before long, he was sitting before tall crackling flames that illuminated the grove in dancing shadows.

He sat cross-legged before the *fyr*. In the dirt at his feet, with his shortsweord, he drew from his memory a map of the coastline, the forests, and the mountains. Then he guessed at the place where the cliffs of Trollveggen might be. The raiders would be watching the ports, King Olaf's men, the land trails.

He drew a long peninsula, from northeast to southwest, a long jut of land protruding into the sea. He stared at it, waiting for a plan to come.

He drew a line in the dirt around it, marking the path of the ship that might carry Lina. They would burn the boats ahead of him, and watch the shore. He knew that part of the coast. It would take them three weeks to sail around it. He drew another line straight through the jut. He could make it there before them. He would have to. They would not expect him. Two-thirds up the line he jabbed the point of his sweord into the ground and stared at it.

He spoke aloud to himself, "The valley of the ice lakes." He would have to cross it...

The flames reflecting on the blade of his sweord caught his eye. He took it and turned it flat across his knees, the sweord's blade across his left palm and its hilt in his right.

Now, as Helga drifted beyond the reach of his heart, he made his sweord his only hearth-companion. He watched the flames dance on the bright surface, hoping to find in their reflection some partial answer, some memory, however distant, that might provide a clue, or help him remember some small part of a story told by the elders that might let him understand what was happening. Next to him was the *fyr*, the wood crackling and warm, and beyond, there was the darkness, the unending silence and a cold that now he could not seem to escape.

Between him and that lay his sweord, dealing death, and giving him life, giving him, now, this next breath, and the will to go on.

Then in his sweord's reflection, he saw again the burning funeral ship floating before him, and remembered Aleric, the chieftain, the great man he had killed. He remembered looking into the eyes of the man he had first known as an elder when he was only a boy, the man who had sometimes shared with him his wisdom, or sparred with him, encouraging him, too well.

And then all vanished again into the *fyr*.

An owl called from a nearby tree. He was thankful for the sound of another life. He picked up a stone and began to sharpen his sweord's edge. It was all he could think about now. He would follow his sweord, wherever it led. And wherever it led, he would make that his path.

As he drew the stone back and forth across the edge, he saw his hands, calloused but not bloody, his feet, the same. The deep cut on his forearm had closed completely and seemed to be healing. He had no other wounds.

Still, he was exhausted, now only acting out the old memories in his body, sharpening his sweord, breaking wood for the *fyr*, things he knew to do without thinking, as though he could assemble these actions into some semblance of his former self. But the image was distorted and incomplete, as in a shattered mirror, with shards uneven and lost, more like a reflection in a stream than a pond, never fully forming, only swirling and moving downstream, leaving nothing behind but a dark still pool.

Maybe they would sell his daughter into slavery. He might never find her then. She would be a concubine until she was killed. He tried to sense their intentions.

Pain shot through his forefinger. A drop of blood had formed where he had been feeling his sweord's edge. It was good. The edge was good, he thought.

* * *

The night came upon Helga. She was moving through the forest listening to every sound. She felt better to be returning to the coast, and someone who might help her, but she knew she needed to conserve her strength for the long march tomorrow. She looked for a patch of thick trees and brush, anywhere she might find some protection from the night cold. She found a hollow beneath a rock outcropping, and lay down, brushing the leaves over her.

Through the branches, she could see the stars hanging in the night sky. The night was growing colder, and her body heat was growing less as her body rested. She pushed the cold away from her, and tried to reach out to feel Lina. She knew she was still alive. She willed her strength into her daughter, as she spoke through the stars, "Your father is coming, Lina..."

* * *

Hearing the call of a hawk, Gundar looked up to see it flying overhead – his senses sharpened and he listened. He could not hear them yet, but he knew they were coming – how many? If he could make it back to the shore, he could follow them by sea, choosing the place of his landing. This they knew. They would try to stop him before he reached it.

He watched the warriors pass on the trail below. One by one, then two by two, they were marching. He studied them, watched their pace, and their rhythm. He watched their eyes, following the path of their vision, left and right, forward and back, man-to-man, looking for a way to approach, a place to strike. But there was nowhere. Not here. Not now. Not yet.

He surveyed the landscape. Nearby was a steep slope ending in a sharp edge of rock over a forty-foot ravine, enough to kill a man. He would have to lead them there. He was exhausted but he steeled himself, forcing his will into his blood and muscles.

Within seconds, he was slashing down saplings, hacking the ends to spear points. When he had five, he bundled them under an arm, and strode to a thick clump of brush halfway up the incline. He grabbed large stones, some for throwing sound, some for killing.

He felt himself an animal alone in the wilds. He knew nothing but survival, and the stalking of prey.

At last he stopped, squatting in the brush, listening to the heaving of his own breath. He let his breathing quiet, until he could hear the sounds of the forest again, and now, the distant broken sound of men marching. He listened harder, trying to separate the sounds, three, four, more, maybe ten, twelve warriors. Maybe they had split into groups to find him.

He planned to slay twelve, one by rock, maybe three by spear, eight by sweord. Eight by sweord...no, it would be late in that battle...he would be weary...it was too many, but he was running out of time to set his trap. He ran to the edge of the ravine and looked down – a good drop. He spotted a large flat rock three feet across and a large natural protrusion where someone might stand to survey the ravine below.

With his sweord, he loosened stones to make a deep cut in the cliff edge. Then, straining himself beyond any earthly strength, he moved a great flat rock over it. The stone was too big. He pulled it away to hack the cut wider, and replaced the stone so only the thinnest ledge of loose rock and earth held it.

It would be his sign. Here the battle would begin.

One more warrior would die here. That left eleven, still too many. He heard the sound of marching coming nearer. Then eleven it would be, but at least ten would die taking him. He went back to his spot in the brush. As he stared down as his spears, he had a thought. He grabbed the strongest one and sharpened it so it had a point on each end. Then he held it by its middle and felt the weight.

He knew his father's teachings were in him, but he could not bring them to his mind. He only hoped his body remembered, from those long years of training. Help me now, father, he thought, or I will be seeing you too soon in Valhalla.

He calmed himself as the marching drew nearer. He looked at his stones. He grabbed a smooth one and looked in the direction of the trail. He leaned his spears on a rock, laying the double-ended one to one side, his sweord to the other.

He began to quiet himself, more and more deeply. He listened to the wind in the branches, looked at the broken sunlight on the leaves, bringing himself to focus on the present moment. What little his life meant now, it could not be lost, or Lina would be lost and he would have failed Helga. No, he would not die today.

Gundar waited, and when the time came, he threw the rock toward the trail. The marching stooped. He threw another rock. They were entering the wood. One more – he tossed it to the halfway mark in the slope. It knocked some other stones and a few slid down the hill. Good.

The warriors raced up the slope. Seeing nothing, they approached the cliff's edge. One began to step on the flat rock. As his weight touched the stone, a spear passed through the chest of the man next to him. As his companion swung round, the stone gave way underneath his feet, plunging him to his death. As the other men turned, Gundar let fly two more spears, killing two more. The others began rushing him. He grabbed his double-ended spear and his sweord and began running sideways across the slope, drawing them to one side. As the first two approached, he rushed between them, holding his spear at gut level and, putting one knee to the ground to steady himself, thrust first one end and then the other into the bellies of the two men, who dropped to the ground, dying miserably.

Even his anger could not stop him from relieving the men of their agony, which he did with a swift thrust of his sweord to their hearts. That left six.

He grabbed a handful of gravel to rub into his hands and dry the slippery blood. From above, a warrior with battleaxe held high leaped down from the rock above. Before his feet hit the ground, Gundar swung his sweord through his leg severing it at the knee, and pivoting, struck his back with a killing blow as the warrior landed and toppled.

Two warriors rushed up the hill toward him from his right side. In a single motion, Gundar whipped his shortsweord from his belt and let it fly into the man's chest. He used the slope to give him advantage as he struck a great downward stroke through the helmet of the other warrior, cleaving through his brain.

Gundar's breath burned cold in his throat. He grabbed his shortsweord from the fallen warrior's chest and began racing sideways down the slope, a sweord in each hand. Blood frenzy moved him beyond exhaustion into the last minute of a battle. Crossing his sweords before his chest, he fell amongst them, letting his sweords fly outward with his arms as he slashed two warrior's throats and then brought both sweords down upon and through the shoulders of the remaining man. Gundar fell to his knees with him as he died, holding himself from collapsing completely to the ground by holding onto the sweords buried in his shoulders, as the man fell to his knees, and then fell dead. Gundar's lungs heaved and the blood splatter on his face ran down into his eyes.

He looked around at the trees and nothing was moving, and there was no wind and no sound. All dead, these lives, these men...still, there was only Thor, only Lina.

With his hand, Gundar wiped the blood from his face, and wept.

* * *

On his longship, Goth discussed Helga's flight with Vakr.

"We have word of her going inland," advised Vakr.

"She will return to the coast, to someone she knows, or Gundar knows..." Goth replied. "Find the ship's owner. Get a list of all those who sailed, and those that returned. Pay him in gold if you have to."

Vakr was surprised. "Good sailing men are hard to find. What if he will not give us the list?"

"Take a lot of gold. Buy his ship if you have to." Goth answered, impatient. "Then go to the villages along the coast. Say you need men for a voyage. Tell them you have heard of Gundar, and want to speak to the man who might best know of him. That is where his woman will go. When you find her, put a sweord through her heart. Nothing else. Understand?"

"As you bid," Vakr said.

Goth continued. "We will put you ashore with six men. There."

Goth pointed toward a large bay encircled by four villages, then looked over his shoulder to see Lina staring at him from far back in the ship, as though she had heard.

"That child is possessed," Vakr warned.

"She is his blood," Goth acknowledged, staring at her and wondering if Vakr was right.

* * *

In a vast timber hall, with a dozen smaller halls attached, the man who called himself King Olaf sat on a great wooden throne before three hundred of his finest warriors. He has found the recent news from his lands disturbing.

"And now this outlaw threatens me in my own kingdom?" King Olaf asked a priest.

"Gundar Avangarsson. He has slain Aleric and taken the sacred scrolls of the Holy Church," the priest answered. "Hundreds are dead!"

"Does he raise an army?" Olaf asked.

"He is ghost. We do not know how many fight with him," the priest replied.

"A ghost? We will soon see if he is. Find him and kill him. And his blood," King Olaf said, turning to a chieftain called Asgar Long Arm. "Take fifty of your men," and then, reflecting further, "make it a hundred. And try to come back with at least fifty of them."

* * *

Gundar walked down the slope toward the stream. He waded into it, and began washing the blood from his legs and arms. He did it without thinking, without feeling, exhausted from all feeling, or beyond it. He did not know how many more battles he could fight.

He was hungry. All his strength was gone, and he realized he had not eaten in a day. He knew he had to keep moving, make every minute count, but he had to eat if he was to go on. He decided to hunt.

He waded out of the stream, picked up his bow, and began moving silently through the forest, listening to every sound.

Finally, after more than an hour, he heard movement. He stopped, listened, looked around. Only thirty yards away a large seven-point buck stood on the ridge. Silently, he drew his bow and fixed an arrow, taking aim. The buck turned its head, sensing something. Gundar had a clear shot behind the left shoulder. The buck looked at him. He saw its eyes. But his mind was racing, and his arms were weak. He released. The shot missed and the buck bounded off. It did not matter. He had no time or strength to slaughter it. A *fyr* would attract attention. There was other food, hares, more difficult to shoot with bow and arrow, but he could try. He would have to wash the meat in a stream. The small hares would be easier to clean and wash, and to eat raw. He had done it before.

He strung another arrow and began stepping through the forest growth. He bound himself to the task, and before nightfall, he was sitting by the stream, cleaning the fur off two large hares. He had changed his mind about the danger and had built a small carefully laid *fyr* to cook the meat.

After he had eaten, he separated the wood in his *fyr*, and let the flames fade into embers. The glowing globe of firelight diminished and the night grew cold around him, as the last few sparks flew into the night sky. He tried not to think of Thor, or Helga, only how he would find Lina, and get her back.

After he ate, he curled up in his garments and slept.

In the bright sun of morning, the mist was rising from the ground frost as smoke from a *fyr*. He rubbed his hands and stomped his feet to warm them from the harsh night cold. There would be many more nights ahead, and many colder.

He had not wanted to leave Helga, but the kidnappers were putting distance between him and his daughter, and Helga had so chosen.

The path was west and then north. To the cliffs of Trollveggen, the warrior had told him. They would sail with her. They would take his daughter north. It would take them more than a week to round the point. They would be guarding the coast, and the ships, looking for him.

He would have to go inland, and it would save him time. He would have to cross the peninsula mountains on foot. The valley of the ice lakes, too, he would have to cross. No one had crossed them. Many had tried. None had lived. But it was not this day's *weorc* and he put it from his mind.

Gundar beheld the great icy mountains ahead, ridge behind ridge, a staircase into the blue horizon. He knew there were passes, valleys, forests. These he could cross. It would be a long march. There was not time to waste.

Ahead, the ice lakes waited.

CHAPTER SEVEN

THE WASTELAND

Soon the first week of marching had turned into two. Freezing days became icier nights. The land grew higher and higher above the ocean, rising into great cliffs higher than fifty masts, and the coastal plateaus grew drier, and emptier, deep forests rising into rock strewn plains of ice and snow.

Even in the trees, this forest was without water now. No streams. The snow did not melt and run because of the cold. The steady winds dried out the forest floor. As he walked, even the branches he stepped on cracked like dry bones.

He left the mountain's edge and descended into the lower valleys. At night, he passed like a solitary wolf through the outskirts of seaside villages. Always downwind, moving silently, he slipped past the stone and stave huts, so even the dogs could not sense his passing.

At times, in the distance through the woods, he could see the villagers through the windows of their cottages, in the light of their fires. It was a life that had been stolen from him, a life he might never know again.

Always he watched from afar, catching a few glimpses, as though stealing glances through a broken wall. These villagers seemed content with their way. Perhaps here it had been a generation or more since there had been a raid or war. Perhaps for them those were just stories now told by the elders around the lodge fires. As in the village where he was born, they would mark their time on earth by the seasons of their crops, and the birth of their children, and the passing of the elders. He marked the passage of time now by the number of times he would stop to rest between dusk and dawn, or the streams that he crossed.

Always he stopped to drink, not knowing when the next stream would come, yet certain water could never quell his thirst. It fell into his belly as drops of rain into a dry lakebed.

Once in the evening, passing by an outdoor gathering around a bonfire, he heard singing. He could not make out the song they were singing, and it all seemed so strangely out of place in the dull gray world that had become his. They were of this earthly life – a life he could only hope to one day join again.

Music lived on without him, and he without it. He wondered if he ever would be able to feel it again, feel anything with the least part of joy. Then the night would come again. The red and golden sun would drop into the low clouds, or sometimes, on a clear day, disappear in a flash of green. Then the creatures that hunted in the darkness hunted again. He felt himself one of them, at once prey and predator.

The trail brought him to the crest of the hills. When he looked out, the sky above the valley below was churning with rising clouds of black smoke. Far below, he saw a village burning in a hundred great fires scattered over the valley floor. The church, the houses, the fields, all was aflame. He knew too well it had been raided.

The village was in his path. He would have to pass through it to continue his journey north.

By late afternoon, he had arrived. Black smoke filled the air, burning his throat and nostrils with his every breath. He covered his mouth and nose with his arm, but it was of no use. He had to make his way through and beyond the acrid air.

All around him, the thatched roofs of the huts were aflame and collapsing. The pathways were empty. He saw no villagers. He began to sense this was not an ordinary raid. Things that should have been taken lay everywhere, saddles, tools, blankets, metal plates, even a sweord. No, this was something different. Something else had happened here. He knew he would find no food or shelter here. The barking and howling of dogs hastened him on.

Suddenly, approaching the next cottage, something caught his eye. A large and valuable tapestry had been hung between two posts driven into the ground. As he approached it, his astonishment and his wariness grew. When he reached it, he was certain. The tapestry belonged to him, taken from his cottage.

It must be the same raiders then, but why this sign? It was a message to him, but what message? That they knew he was following? As he looked back at the village, he sensed and feared this violence and destruction had been done on his account, and a sickness churned in his stomach. Behind the tapestry was a stone cottage that had not been burned. Another message?

He drew his sweord and entered, stepping over a dead man lying face down in the doorway. Seeing no one there, he sheathed his sweord and began looking for water. He looked everywhere, turning over every bowl and vessel, but not a single bowl had been left untouched. There was no water. They were making his way hard. Why did they not just wait and kill him? There was no ambush here when there could have been.

The sound of muffled weeping intruded into his thoughts, coming from an adjoining room in the cottage. He stepped through a small archway and looked around.

There was a bed made from a pile of black and white reindeer furs. He drew his shortsweord and approached cautiously. The fur was moving, rising and falling with someone's breathing.

He slowly lifted it. The naked girl underneath began screaming wildly. He placed his hand on her arm to calm her, until gradually her screaming became great sobs and wailing.

He could see she was not more than thirteen. Her pretty peasant face was blue and bruised, and there was blood between her legs. He pulled the fur back over her, and stroked her hair. He took a couple of strips of dry meat hanging from his belt and placed them on the wooden stump next to her.

Suddenly an elderly woman rushed at him swinging a heavy stick.

"Evil! Evil!" she screamed. "Evil!"

He blocked the blows with his arm.

"I do not harm her!" he said.

But the old woman heard nothing, "Get out! Get out!" she screamed, striking at him again with the stick.

Seeing there was nothing he could do, Gundar slipped out of the back of the cottage, back into the bright sunlight that had broken through the smoke.

What lay outside was worse. Through the glare and smoke, he could see the raiders had made a pile of bodies, thirty or forty men and women. His heart pounded in his chest but he did not turn his face away. Two nearby buildings exploded into a firestorm of raging flames, scorching the air and burning the backs of his hands and neck. He lifted his fur robe over his head and made his way away from the burning village, still thinking of what he had seen.

He crossed an open field, toward the forest. At its edge, he found a young man standing over a weeping woman sitting in the grass, a dead man lying before her. The young man looked at him in fear, but Gundar held his hand up in friendship, showing it held no weapon. The young man turned his eyes back to the woman, who seemed to be his mother.

"My father tried to stop them. They killed him," the young man said.

Gundar looked upon the weeping woman and the dead man.

"I am sorry," Gundar said.

"We will leave," the young man answered. "The son of Eric the Red, Leifr Eiriksson, has taken a ship west to a new land."

"West? To Iceland?" Gundar asked.

"Beyond. Beyond Greenland."

"What is beyond Greenland?" Gundar wanted to know.

"A new land, they say. Not like here. A place to live in peace," the young man said.

"You can make your family there?" Gundar asked, drawn in.

But the young man said nothing. He was not really speaking to Gundar, only giving voice to his thoughts. He kneeled down to the woman. "Come away, mother," he said. "Come away."

Gundar hesitated for a moment, watching them depart, and then walked on, entering the forest.

His thoughts were disturbed. He had known war. He had seen death, in many forms. But when they raided, when *he* raided with his ship-companions, they rushed through the villages and were gone in minutes.

They were there for plunder, not harm, only taking what they wanted by whatever means necessary. He realized, though, he had never seen the aftermath of his own attacks, and he could not get the image of the young screaming girl out of his mind.

More images began flashing in his mind, images of his own raiding. He had not killed woman or children, but he had seen others kill them. He had never raped. He had seen others rape, many women, some girls. He had wanted no part of it, but he had remained silent. He could not remember speaking against it. It disturbed him now that he had not. He wondered if he would ever join a raid again.

He would have to find another way. If he could have his family again, if the gods would allow him...maybe the boy was right...maybe in a new land, across the sea. First, he would have to find out who was making war upon him, and upon his family.

The trail and days ahead brought more of the same. It was only a few days before he crossed another peak to come upon another village, burning as before. And each day, as he crossed another valley, or reached the peak of another hill, he saw smoke rising before him, another village burning. There was no food, no water, no hearth, no comfort or sustenance. He took what water he could find from the dew on the needles of the pine trees. They meant to take everything from him. He could see that now.

They were watching the coast, marking his way with death and burning. He had only one choice. He would have to go inland. He would have to cross the ice lakes.

He began marching for days. At times, when his day's journey was over, as the sun touched the horizon and the low shadows of trees began to blend into the darkness of night, he would think of Helga. Between the hard labor of his march, and the coming coldness of night, he would remember her, and the moments they shared...the red sunsets over the seashore as she walked beside him with her graceful stride, the curves of her strong shoulders... She was there somewhere, in this night, in this wind.

But his thoughts of her only tormented him. He was sure he could feel her anger, her hardness of heart. He wondered if she would she ever forgive him. He wondered if her love would ever be the same, or only half-return, like the sun behind the clouds, there but not warm, its light broken, not bright.

He stared at the stones at his feet, black and brown and gray, some smooth, some shiny, some rough, as though they might speak and give him some answer.

Now cliffs were below him, on the sea, and cliffs were above him, to the horizon. There would be caves now, some brief shelter from the night. In that world of rock and stone he would be alone, to find his strength, or lose it.

He made his way toward the cliffs above, to find his home for the night. Too exhausted to build a *fyr*, he collapsed into sleep only to awaken into a half-dream. He was sure he was awake, but he could not move. His arms and legs were as though dead, not part of his will. He could not speak. So when she appeared in the mouth of the cave he could not even cry out. He wanted to reach for her.

"Will you live, Gundar?" she whispered.

It was as though he was listening to the conversation, not joining it.

"Will you live even as Thor is gone," she said, "and you may not have another?"

He could say nothing. What was her tone? Condemnation? Despair? Prophesy? Or her own refusal to begin again? He prayed for deeper sleep, not for release from his pain, but for a change of worlds, not knowing whether another would be better than this.

When he awoke, it was the same. The morning was gray and damp. The wetness dripped from branches. His mind filled with the same thoughts. His body rose. His feet moved him.

He marched. He did not know what were worse now, the dreams that came by night to torment him, or the ones that came by night to haunt him. At night, he could escape the angry night visions by waking into the darkness, and the cold forest of still trees, but by day that same warring sleep seemed it might prove his only escape from the dark turnings of his mind. So he fled, and was pursued from one strange darkness into another as each tried to hold him in its grasping hands, escaping one only to fall deeper into the other.

If he had known another way, he would have followed it. There was nothing for him to do but to go on, moving with each day, hoping the darkness would not overtake him.

Every day he marched from early dawn to twilight. He made fires when he could. His body led, because his mind was weakening. He walked through the wind and under the sky and it was all he knew. He spoke with them because there was no one else to speak with, wondering if the turnings of his own heart and gut were painting the sky with his own turmoil. If he could only take the sky in his fist and crush it into fragments of white and blue stone to throw into the Northern sea, he might disgorge the cutting razor pain in his belly to banish it into a night a thousand years hence, and so escape the vicious god that now held his heart hostage.

He marched on, while the blue sky above him was darkening with red, like a river of blood pouring into a lake. All beneath it lay under its crimson spell, because like a wounded animal he only wanted to kill now, kill all that came near.

Nights became dreams, became wars, became his living world, only partially relieved by dawn. He could follow the sun, or follow the moon and the moonless night. Day became more a dream, the haunting of a brief reality he no longer wanted to endure.

So as though turning from a disturbing sight, he changed the dream of day. In this new day, he had no wife, no son, and no daughter. Then those harsh shadows could not torment and taunt him, challenging with his own failures his will to prevail. So when the light of morning came each day he held on to it. It was for him now the first light, the light of creation. It made his march possible. It made all possible.

When a day of rain would come, although he did not want to slow, or let his mind and spirit rest, he did, because, he knew he had to. He knew he would need to renew himself, if he was going to find the strength for the battles ahead. Then he let the stillness of the trees in the still day be his guide. He resolved not to let exhaustion stalk and overtake him.

He chose a rhythm. Five hours of marching, one hour of rest. Then when twilight came, he would force himself to build a *fyr* and grow strong again in its warmth. He would hunt and eat meat. He would force his mind and spirit to rest, to be with the still trees and the rain dripping from their branches, watching the mists swirl and shift almost invisibly between shades of gray and white as they drifted over the forest floor and amongst the branches.

Lina. Maybe they would not throw her from the cliffs. Would they give that death to a child? Or sell her into slavery? Where she would be a concubine until she was killed, or he found her? Whatever would be, he vowed to kill their leader slowly.

The days grew into weeks.

So often, he thought the light would come – that the night would pass and another day begin anew. But then the gray sky would be lit only dimly and the same day would return with no more hope or grace than those dim skies above would admit. Helga was gone. Even in his heart he could not find her. Not because he did not hold her there, but because when he reached out for her, there was only the grayest silence.

And into that silence rushed shadows, like autumn fields and November frost, bringing memories, or were they dreams, that fell upon him, one after another, day into night, glistening, then dark, stealing his breath to make their own story...until his life had become no more than a deserted temple, where the phantom of a priest passed without speaking, to catch its vestments on a splinter of wood, leaving only threads.

Through the cold days and icy nights, the furs he wore became more like his own thickening skin, the animals that once owned them reclaiming their spirit in his. When at night he stopped in the bright moonlight to drink from the still pool of a stream, he saw in the water a face more animal than human. It was an animal he knew, one he had kept at bay all his life but now was growing stronger within him.

It was the animal of the battle frenzy and the slaughter. It was the animal that took what it wanted and killed all those that opposed it. How many more days would it be before it was the only thing left inside him? Would it help him to victory? Help him find his daughter, find a new life with Helga? And when he had these, would there be anything of him left to go on, that he had not forever given to that beast?

CHAPTER EIGHT
FINDING SKL'ULI

Helga had reached the forest's edge, where the fields of the village began. It was dusk. The forest was growing dark, and the villagers were retreating into their huts. It was a large village of more than a hundred cottages. She did not know where to begin to find Skuli.

In front of her, in a field, a man and woman passed, pulling a cart of straw.

"You have not dried enough meat for the winter," the man said.

"You have not given me enough." the woman replied, to which the man grunted as they moved on.

Suddenly she heard running footsteps and laughter. It was two children, a young boy and girl, running right toward her. They crashed through the tall grass, almost running into her.

They stopped, frightened, and began walking back away from her.

"Wait, children," Helga said, "Wait."

The children stopped.

"I am Helga. It's all right," Helga said, in a calm and reassuring voice.

"You don't live here," the boy said.

"No, but I am looking for someone from here. A man named Skuli. Do you know him?"

"Everyone knows Skuli!" the young girl exclaimed.

The boy, deciding she was good, took her hand and led her toward the village center, telling the girl, "Come on, Marta, we will show her."

Skuli recognized Helga when she knocked on his door. He opened it, exclaiming, "Thank the gods you are all right," he said, embracing her and ushering her into his home.

Soon, she was sitting with Skuli in front of the glowing flames of his stone hearth as his wife bought cooked fish and potatoes. Skuli was tending the *fyr*, pushing the logs around with an iron poker.

"We heard the tidings. These are terrible times, Helga. I am sorry about Thor," Skuli said.

"The Gods have taken my son, Skuli. Gundar angered them with the scrolls," Helga said.

"It is men that killed Thor, Helga," Skuli replied.

"Men that came for the scrolls," Helga answered. She took a long breath. "I only want my daughter back now. Will you help him?"

"I will find Gundar, and we will bring her back, Skuli replied."

Helga nodded. "I pray to Odin for her safe return."

"And Gundar's?" Skuli asked, sensing her anger.

"I cannot pray for him," Helga said.

Then she turned away, knowing her anger toward Gundar wrong. "I cannot."

Skuli went to a wooden chest, removed a small bag of coins, and put them on the table before her.

"Go north to Ravndal. Gundar will meet you there with Lina."

"Then I pray to the gods for you, Skuli," Helga, said.

* * *

100

CHAPTER NINE

THE RIVER OF WOLVES

Gundar had been counting the days. He did not know if he could maintain his pace. The climate was growing harsher, each day, shorter. The sun was already falling dim behind a thick layer of clouds when suddenly he heard a louder movement in the brush – footsteps, but not a man's.

He continued walking for a few more steps and then stopped. It stopped. He listened harder. There was silence, but he knew it was listening, too. It had stopped because he had stopped. He began to walk again. The falling footsteps followed him. It was stalking him. He stopped again and waited to see if it had stopped. When he heard no more footsteps, he began to move a few steps as silently as possible to gain some distance. Then he burst into a run, but listening to the footsteps following him, he realized it was easily keeping pace with him. He was being stalked. Through the forest, he heard a wolf howling. Then another. Now their steady loping, panting, and hoarse growling surrounded him on all sides.

The one following him most closely was only ten yards away, waiting for more to join it before attacking. He could not outrun them, but he kept running, trying to think. He realized they were pushing him toward the cliff's edge, cornering him. He heard the nearest wolf closing the distance.

Suddenly, it cleared the brush. He stopped and turned, gazing at it, but not meeting its eyes – he knew that would provoke an immediate attack. The enormous black wolf, its shoulders as high as his waist, bared its fangs in dripping jaws. It stood its ground as he did his, its steady growling filling his ears.

He slipped his bow from around his shoulder and notched his arrow. Just as suddenly, another wolf appeared closer off to his left. Snarling, it leaped for him as he dropped his bow to pull his shortsweord. He thrust it into the wolf's chest as the wolf sank its fangs into his shoulder.

The second wolf was upon him so fast he had only time to thrust his forearm into its jaws to protect his face and throat. As it bit through his leather armguard, he fell back, wrapping his other arm around the wolf's neck. With a violent jerk, he thrust the wolf's head back, snapping its neck. It collapsed on him with its full weight. He threw it off him, stood, and swung his sweord in time to slash at another leaping wolf. He could hear more wolves coming to join the hunt. He threw down his shortsweord, and pulled out his longsweord, circling it to mark a radius around him as he backed up.

In seconds, more wolves attacked. He slashed the first with his sweord, pulling his knife to plunge it into another's belly, even as a searing pain shot through his left arm, as the wolf ripped through his tunic into the flesh of his forearm. He ripped his knife back through the wolf's stomach as another attacked his leg. He struck it on the back of his neck with the butt of his sweord, as its fangs tore wildly at his flesh.

The river – it was his only chance, if he could make it. Again, he slammed his sweord down hard on the back of the wolf's neck, and it dropped, releasing him. The wolf on his arm finally fell dead. He looked to the river, not taking the time to calculate the distance. Dropping his longsweord, putting his knife into his belt and grabbing his shortsweord off the ground, he ran.

He heard more wolves running behind him, closing on him. He ran until his breath burned in his chest and he felt his legs weakening. With his last bit of will, he pushed his strength into his failing muscles to keep driving his pace, even as they gained on him and the sound of their running grew loud in his ears.

Finally, he reached the river canyon, and began to run along side it. Sixty feet below, he saw a deep pool in the middle of the river. With a wolf leaping after him, he jumped.

He plummeted toward the water, breaking through the branches, the wolf falling with him. He hit the water, plunging into a deep pool, while the wolf fell behind him, hitting the sharp rocks, and dying instantly.

He submerged into the icy river, striking his feet hard on the gravel bottom. The raging current tumbled him through the roiling water, slamming him against the rocks, twisting him in one direction and then another. He put his arms overhead to ward them off as he pushed his head above the surface, choking and coughing out the churning water.

He watched the riverbank pass, desperately searching for a way out of the rushing water. The cold was reaching through his muscles into his bones. He felt his limbs growing sluggish. He was losing control of his muscles, and knew he would drown in minutes.

Ahead, he saw a large limb dipping into the water. Summoning his last bit of strength, he raised his arms to it, hitting it so hard it knocked the wind from him. The water pinned him against the limb as he pulled himself toward the shore, scraping his arms against the coarse bark.

Finally, the water slowed around him, and he was able to reach the riverbank. He dug his hands, hand over hand, into the gravel of the river's edge, using all his strength to pull himself onto the stony bank. He laid face down on the cold stony ground, his body trying to warm itself with his every breath, fighting for life.

When the least bit of strength finally returned to his limbs, he began to crawl. He hardly had the strength to lift his head and look up the bank. He forced his way through the brush, to the flat ground between the roots of a great oak, and rolled over onto his back.

He felt around his chest and belly. The waxed leather pouch was still there. He opened it to feel inside. Miraculously, the scrolls were only damp. His seafaring ways had saved them. The priests would still be able to read the marks. Somehow, it comforted him.

He looked up through the leaves of the huge branches above him to the last broken light of the sun, glowing gold and red below the high mountain horizon, as he brushed its dry fallen leaves over his body, hoping he would live to morning, wondering if this would be the last thing he ever saw.

As the shivering subsided, in his last moments before sleep, or unconsciousness, he saw Helga smiling, walking, half-dancing, as he remembered her when he had first met her, so lithe, so spirited. He wondered if he would he ever see her again.

Halfway through the night he awoke into a bitter cold, the dampness icy on his skin, his clothes freezing on him. He did not know how many hours had passed, or whether he had slept or been unconscious. He was shivering hard now, and the shivering started to become a violent shuddering through his whole body. He did not know how long it was before dawn. He tried to hang on.

There was a damp madness in the air, a slithering chaos that clung to every branch and rock and pushed its bony fingers into his freezing flesh. Strange and changing shapes in the rocks made them seem alive, moving as his eyes moved. These mountains were not for men. He wanted to be at sea, dying a death he knew, with the gods he sailed with. This forest realm for him held only dark gods, lords of unknown worlds. He knew if he lingered here, they would come to know him too well, tormenting him through this world and on into the next.

From the dark sky came hard rain and sleet, and the wind began blowing, the drops striking him like knives. He knew he would not last another day out here.

The river rushed loud in his ears, as he felt the ground damp reaching up to claim his legs. If he fell asleep again, he knew the cold would kill him while he slept. He shook his head, trying to clear his vision and his mind, but failed. The cold held him in its fierce grip. He pulled his long knife from its sheath, reached up and buried it at arm's length into a tree. He dragged himself closer, and tried to pull himself up. A dagger of pain shot through his back and leg. He stopped to breathe, and to ease the pain. Then he pulled again, dragging himself up to standing.

He would have to find a cave, or a stand of rocks. His breath clouded and fell as crystals at his feet. Enough of land. He had to get back to the sea. He would take a boat. The sea was all he knew. He could build one if he had to. How long would that take him? How many of the locals would oppose him before they gave up? He would have to kill at least thirty of them, to have time to build his boat. No, more would come then. He would have to kill all the men in the village, whoever fought him. Would the women come for revenge if he killed the men? The children, would they fight? His thoughts were falling one atop the other, losing sense.

On the distant ridge in the dark and the fog, the sky opened with a crack of thunder that exploded into another crash, and another, until he thought the heavens themselves had broken. The rumbling seemed to last for minutes, rolling through his body and his mind. Not ordinary thunder, thought Gundar, but the rage of the gods, and the threat of the end times – Ragnorak.

He could not stop the shaking in his body. He knew his thoughts were unclear. There was not much time now. He had to find shelter. He would have to go down to the next village, and hope Goth's men had not been there, to turn the people against him.

He should have waited until the light had broken, but he brushed off his cover of leaves, as though he could shake the cold from his bones, and set off. He only knew he could not survive out here now.

He found a trail and then a stream crossing it. He turned down it into its steep ravine, following its course toward the village, climbing, sliding, and leaping down the wet boulders.

As he descended, he saw there were new landscapes now, low ranges of hills sloping into green valleys, cut by cliff-lined fjords with the blue ice of glaciers behind, winding back up into the green and black mountains.

He descended, even as his burning muscles stiffened into clay.

He descended, as his feet grew sore from slamming into the rock with each leap or slide, bringing him with each move, closer to the world of men.

* * *

On his longship Goth stood on the deck beneath the luffing sail, speaking to Hakon, eating a piece of fruit as the ship pounded through the heavy waves. He was wearing an enormous black bearskin, its claws covering his shoulders and its huge head atop his head. He wore it for power, and for his own amusement.

"He will die if he tries to cross the ice lakes," Hakon advised.

"Then our story might be over," Goth agreed, but he has more to live for than himself," adding, "Destroy the boats in the villages ahead. "Then we will visit him in Raumalen, where he must go."

Goth knew the sea would comfort Gundar, and allow him to grow stronger. "A gold piece for each one you burn. These villagers are not our enemy, and there is no reason to make them so." For the time being, Goth was feeling more in control.

Hakon nodded in agreement, but Goth did not see. Goth slapped Hakon's arm with the back of his hand.

"Right?"

"It's your gold, Goth," Hakon replied.

"My gold..." Goth mused.

For a moment, as the ship rode on, carried by its sixty oars, Goth looked up into the coastal mountains, as though knowing Gundar's hardships.

"Stay alive, Gundar," he yelled across the sea into the far mountains, and then speaking for himself, "Stay alive, so that one day we might finish this."

CHAPTER TEN

THE POWER OF FYR

The women working in the fields saw him first. He saw one lean over to a young boy who then ran toward the village center. Soon a dozen armed men stood on the road twenty feet before him, armed with axes, scythes, and pitchforks.

He stopped. He was freezing and exhausted. The only thing he could think to do was to hold up a hand in friendship. He knew he could not fight them all. Now, he could not fight anyone. He had no sweord and no strength. And he did not want to kill the innocent.

He walked slowly forward, making no sudden moves. As though in a dull dream, in the fog of his freezing bones and blood, he began taking off his empty sweord belts, letting them fall to the ground. He threw his longknife down beside them.

One of the men stepped forward. "Who are you?"

Gundar looked at the man, who seemed to be the headman of the village.

"I search for my daughter who has been taken," Gundar answered simply.

"He's a raider," a voice shouted from the crowd.

"Kill him!" a woman shouted.

"No! It is Gundar Avangarsson."

A murmur went through the crowd, as they all took a step back. Gundar was known as a great warrior throughout the entire land. Gundar could see their fear. It was not what he needed now.

"Gundar of Kallekot." A young woman emerged from the crowd as she spoke, "The son of Avangar."

Gundar looked up to see a tall beautiful woman of eighteen or twenty years with dark brown hair flowing over her bare shoulders, approaching him as the others still watched with mistrust.

"He must be brought to the elders," the headman said.

"No time..." Gundar said, starting to back away. But he faltered, his legs weakening underneath him. The young woman rushed forward to hold him up. She saw the blood running down his leg.

"If he lives," she said sternly.

"My son killed...Helga...my daughter taken..." Gundar struggled with his words, hoping at least one of the villagers might understand.

"Let me tend to him," Eilina said. "Come." She took him away from the angry crowd toward a small cottage.

"They killed him..." Gundar blurted out, hardly coherent, struggling to walk.

"Shhh....There will be time to speak," she assured him while taking gentle command.

"I have to find her..."

Eilina brought Gundar inside a nearby cottage, and laid him on a bed covered with furs near a flaming hearth.

"Rest, rest" she said again.

She carefully laid three more logs into the *fyr*.

"Trollveggen," he uttered, "My daughter."

"You will be warm soon," she added. "Rest."

He watched as she ladled broth from the iron pot hanging in the hearth into a pottery bowl, broke a few pieces of bread into it, and brought it to him.

"It is hot," she warned.

He took it into his hands with a nod and then lifted it to his lips and drank. The heat ran down his throat and into his belly. Now the simple nourishment of food was good. He drank again and the warmth reached his heart. He looked up to see her watching him. He continued sipping, until he felt the warmth replacing the chill in his bones.

"Good," she said. "Now easy...there is time," she advised as he wiped his lips with his hand.

"How are you called?" she asked.

Her voice went right though him, touching him as pure sound, not words.

She waited patiently for him to respond.

Another moment passed.

She smiled.

At last, he heard her words in her mind, 'How are you called?' he heard.

"Gundar," he answered. It was a confession, and an affirmation. "As you have said."

She nodded, and smiled softly.

"Eilina," she gave her name as though giving it back in return for his.

Again her voice, her name, touched him, inside. It was a quiet pronouncement, as though she somehow knew him. She saw him looking at her from a distant place within himself.

"What is it?" she asked.

Gundar said nothing. He was seeing her, but imagining Helga near.

"They say you are a great warrior," she offered.

"How did you know me?" Gundar asked.

"Word spread you were in the mountains. Who else could you be?"

Gundar shook his head slowly. "My son was killed, my daughter taken... I must go, to Trollveggen." He began to sit up.

She came to the bed, and put her hand to his shoulder. "No, you must not strain yourself now. We can speak in the morning."

She was right. He fell back into the furs and sleep overtook him. And for the first time since he had begun his terrible journey, the night passed quickly.

*   *   *

In early morning, as in a dream, he heard a voice. "Gundar?"

He could see no one. The voice came as from another world. "Gundar?" it asked.

Suddenly he awoke, bolting upright to sitting, feeling his chest and belly for the sacred scrolls. They were gone.

"No!" he cried out.

"Wait," a soft but strong voice said.

"My scrolls..."

"They are safe," she assured him. "I have laid them between sheets of wool to dry them."

Awakening more fully, he began to see Eilina was already tending the *fyr*.

"We will eat now," she announced simply.

She slipped out of the cottage and returned after a moment with a handful of eggs and a slab of meat, which she laid carefully in a bowl on the wooden table.

"How do you feel?" she asked.

"Better," he answered, "a little stronger."

Eilina smiled. She cut the meat into thin slices and then put them with the eggs into the iron pan over the *fyr*. They exploded with a sizzle.

"Good. The food will make you even stronger."

Gundar looked at her. "Why did you come forward?"

"Because no one else would," Eilina said plainly, adding, "It is time to eat."

Gundar suddenly realized his tunic had been changed. He rubbed the cloth between his fingers as he looked at it.

"Your tunic was wet as you slept. I put a dry one on."

He looked at her.

She smiled, "Oh, I am stronger than I look. And it was mostly dark," she offered, not without some little humor in her voice.

Gundar was somehow pleased that she had answered both thoughts in his mind without him asking. He rubbed his eyes, stretched his arms behind his head, and looked around at what now seemed new surroundings to him. The morning light illuminated the cottage, making all the colors bright, the brown and silver furs, the green and gold tapestry on the wall, the yellow clay plates. He could see the shining black iron pots hanging over the *fyr* in the stone hearth, and could smell the cooking grain.

Then he looked at her with another question. "You are kind to me?"

"It is our way, Gundar," she said.

"No, it is more," he replied. "Something else…"

"It is not because you are handsome," she answered, teasing him.

With that, he frowned, and then smiled.

Gundar threw off the woolen blankets and sat on the low wooden bench in front of the *fyr*.

While the eggs and pork cooked, she ladled oatmeal from the hanging pot into a large bowl. "You are a large man," she said in a flat tone, keeping her own confidence.

Gundar raised his eyebrows, not sure of her meaning. He wondered why she was being so warm and friendly. He watched her as she added the milk and honey to the steaming oatmeal, realizing how hungry he was.

"Here." She offered him the bowl.

He took it from her and began to eat.

After a moment, she said, "My father makes the rope for the ships you sail on. We trade it up and down the coast."

Gundar said nothing. She could see his mind was elsewhere.

She continued. "My father learned it from his father, and his father from his." She put her hand over his to draw his attention. "It is a very ancient art. Some say more than a hundred generations. I will ask him if I can show you."

With that, Gundar looked up.

"It's a long time, a hundred generations," she said. "Have you ever thought that far into the past?"

Eilina could see the pain in Gundar's face. "Gundar, you will need to stay here for at least a couple of days more."

He shook his head, saying, "I have to go," scraping the last bit of cereal from inside the bowl.

"There is more in the pot," Eilina said.

Gundar looked at the inside of his bowl and suddenly felt embarrassed. He looked at Eilina and they both smiled.

"Try this now." She handed him a plate of scrambled eggs and fried pork.

Eilina stood. "When you finish, come outside."

Eilina disappeared through the doorway. Gundar ate ravenously as she walked outside, glad for the sustenance.

When he emerged into the bright sunlight, he saw Eilina placing a short log on a much larger and wider stump. She skillfully swung her axe overhead and split the log in two, and threw the two halves into her growing pile.

"Ready?" she asked.

"Ready," he answered, noticing Eilina had already split fifteen or twenty logs.

"Come," she said. "I will show you our village." She took his hand and led him outside into the village pathways.

Gundar joined her, walking slowly and with a slight limp.

All the villagers were already hard at *weorc*, each in their own task. Some were on their roofs, repairing the thatch. Some sat on their cottage steps, braiding leather sinew. Others were dying clothes in large vats, the steam rising as many colored clouds into the crisp morning air.

"There is always much to do. Each season has its *weorc* to prepare for the next. Now fall is upon us and soon, winter."

They passed the shed of a leatherworker, where cow and goat hides hung from the rafters, curing in the open air. The man had a fresh hide over his bench and was scraping the fur from it with a wide double-handed knife. Drops of sweat fell from his temples as he labored.

"You have been to villages like ours?" Eilina asked.

Gundar began to feel a little uneasy. He realized it was villages such as these that they sometimes raided when a rich monastery was not to be found.

"Each hide has a different process. It can take many weeks," Eilina continued, overriding his discomfort. "We get back what we give, nothing more."

Gundar nodded, half-listening, wondering if she was trying to tell him something.

The leatherworker looked at him uneasily as though he knew Gundar's thoughts.

They moved on, coming to a bakery, where three large stone ovens stood by the tables and tubs where women kneaded piles of dough.

"They mix rye and barley with the wheat. It makes for a stronger bread," Eilina explained, knowing Gundar was not really listening.

Three woman labored in the tubs with great masses of dough, kneading them and turning them over, using the weight of their bodies to lean their shoulders into the task as they pushed and pulled the great loaves. When they were ready, they were loaded into the ovens with six-foot long flat wooden paddles.

120

The first batch of loaves was already cooling on the table.

Eilina picked a small loaf and broke off a piece. She dipped a wooden knife into a bowl, and then wiped fresh butter over the bread. She handed it to Gundar.

"Taste," she tempted.

He bit into it and the bread was warm and sweet in his mouth.

"This is why we *weorc*," she said simply, taking a bite herself.

They walked on toward the outskirts of the village. They came to a smithy, an open shed where Mord the blacksmith and two other men labored with hammer and anvil, tongs and forge.

On a table just outside, in the sunshine, was a half-covered basket holding a newly born infant, Mord's daughter, and the cause of his wife's recent death in childbirth.

As they strolled past, Eilina explained, "Mord is the master smith. He speaks little now. He lost his wife in childbirth."

As they passed, Mord plunged a newly made scythe into a vat of water, causing hissing steam to blow in a small cloud over the countryside.

Gundar noticed two fine thick-haired horses tied behind the hut.

The smith looked up at him, knowing he was a warrior and a raider. He continued striking with his hammer, but then stopped, and looked at Gundar, knowing he had seen the horses.

He said, "The summers are short, the winters long. The *weorc* is hard. We *weorc* long and eat little." He looked at Gundar, and Gundar knew his meaning.

121

Gundar moved on with Eilina. "Eilina, this place...this village..."

"They still fear you. Come..." Eilina said wisely, taking his arm to move him along. Her spirit was strong and bright, and her limbs graceful as she moved, so that he was able to let go of his thoughts and for a time join his spirit to hers.

Suddenly, from out of the sky, a huge hawk swooped down upon the infant's covered basket, grabbing for the infant.

As those all around gasped in horror, Gundar was already spinning around, whipping his knife from his belt to whip it into the hawks chest, killing it instantly.

Eilina rushed back to the infant to pick it up and put it into Mord's arms. Gundar remained where he stood. Eilina and Mord looked over to him, knowing he had saved the infant's life.

Mord walked to Gundar and said, "I am in your debt."

"No debt is made, Mord. I hope she has a long life," Gundar said as Eilina joined them again.

Mord nodded, shaken and thankful, picking up his child.

Eilina looked at him. She was feeling more than thankful. She felt warmed by his quick action and command.

"Come on," she said, smiling and pulling him along by the hand.

They passed by a cemetery. "My mother and father are buried there. That is where I will go when I die," Eilina pointed out.

Gundar considered it strange that she would say it, and strange that anyone would live and die their whole life in the same place.

The path she was following led through an open field behind the house, toward a large open shed.

His limbs were still stiff, and the morning sun felt good upon him as they walked. They passed a three-year-old boy, playing and dancing with his five-year old sister.

"Speak with them," Eilina suggested.

"Children?" Gundar asked.

"Go on," she cajoled, pushing him toward the children, adding playfully, "You'll think of something."

Gundar approached the children and spoke the first thought that came to him. "Why are you dancing?"

"How come you're not?" the little girl replied.

Gundar stopped, amused, while Eilina strolled along.

The little boy grabbed hold of Gundar's tunic.

"Are you a Viking?" he said, looking up at Gundar as one would a tall tree.

The boy's question caught him by surprise. It was what the villagers called the raiders.

"Are you?" the boy repeated.

"Once I was, a long time ago," Gundar answered.

"Not now?" the boy questioned.

"Not now." Gundar wondered whether he was speaking to the boy or himself. He squatted down to engage the boy further.

"Now I am making new friends. Do you want to be my friend?"

"Talking doesn't make friends," the boy scoffed, as though saying something everyone should know.

"No?" Gundar asked him.

The boy shook his head. Gundar smiled and thought to draw out the boy's thoughts, asking, "What do you mean by that?"

The boy just pressed his lips together and slowly shook his head again, side to side, as though forgiving Gundar for his ignorance, and said knowingly, "You will understand when you grow up to be little like me."

Gundar was taken aback, half-bewildered and half-bemused.

"Gundar," Eilina called to him.

Gundar stood up, still somewhat shocked by the boy's strange wisdom.

Suddenly, as he looked at the child, then toward Eilina, a gust of wind shook a shower of leaves from the trees. As he watched them fall, his mind drifted into the reverie of a better time... his son was in his arms, on his shoulders...he was turning him overhead over and over, as he laughed, his blond hair falling wispy over his eyes...

He strode away to catch up with Eilina, as though he could leave the memory where he stood.

* * *

That night, in her cottage, Eilina gave Gundar venison that she had carefully cooked on a spit over the hearth. As he ate it, thankful for her kindness, he could almost feel the strength of the meat filling him.

Then he winced with the pain in his leg. He checked his bandage, pressed the side of his leg to test the pain. He was more concerned with the healing than with the pain. He wanted to get back on his journey.

When he looked up, she was holding the broken halves of his shortsweord, its shattered blade only a foot long.

"A fisherman found it in the river," she said.

Gundar took the sweord from her, and wrapped it in a blanket, as though embarrassed to have her see it. For some reason, he did not want her to think of him that way.

"And this in the forest nearby," she added.

It was his bow, unstrung, but not broken.

"I thank you," he said, still uncomfortable, adding simply, "I will leave in the morning."

"You will not go far if you do. Your wound will open and a fever will begin."

He believed her, but looked at her for more.

"Another day, maybe two. Here," Eilina said, handing him a shirt of chain mail. "Tidings of your sorrows reached us before you came."

"It was my father's," she said. "He died in it."

He took it respectfully, while knowing she did not like the ways of war.

She continued, "In the mountains, after the lesser trail ends you will find Vindalf. Ask him for a sweord. And then you can begin again."

"Thank you," Gundar said, not knowing what else to say.

"You don't think all women have knowledge of war? We are the ones left behind, with only our stories," Eilina said sadly, and with some bitterness.

* * *

The next day, Gundar found himself again exploring the village with Eilina, his impatience temporarily checked. She was in high sprits, as she skipped ahead, saying, "Here." She disappeared into a long low shed.

He followed. When he entered the shed, he could see there were more than twenty people working there, men and women. Each one seemed absorbed in a different task.

"This is where they prepare the hemp. You see?" Eilina asked.

The long strands of hemp ran down the length of the shed, out into the field. At each end was a twisting crank, to wind the strands together.

He could see now the shed was divided into large sections, with different work underway in each one.

"This," she said, "is the matting station. They soak the hemp first and then they dry it. The building has to be as long as the rope we want to make. It's called a ropewalk. If there was no roof, the rope could only be made in dry weather. It is against the law to sell it to ships if it is wet."

Gundar listened as Eilina continued patiently.

"In May we sow the hemp seed, when the soil is dry," Eilina said, looking at him to see if he was listening.

"We start the harvest now, in the month of August… some of it is ripe, and can be pulled. The male hemp ripens first and it is this that first must be pulled, separate from the female."

She started from one edge of the field, pulling up the ripe hemp in front of her.

"We pull it up with the roots. Try."

Gundar pulled up a few stalks as she watched.

She walked further into the field. "This is how to walk into the field without damaging the plants that remain standing. You see? Come."

He followed her path into the field. She talked as she walked, turning sideways between the rows. "See? Here is the female hemp, the one that bears the seed. It must remain three to four weeks yet to ripen."

She pointed toward some huge piles of cut hemp. "Over there. That's where we prepare it. The children must keep the chickens away, or they'll pick the fibers apart…everyone has a job."

She continued pulling up the hemp, but she knew Gundar's thoughts were elsewhere. She moved toward some huge tubs. "Here we heat the tar. When it is hot enough we pull the rope through." She kept moving. "The soaking makes them strong and supple. We have to be careful. It can catch *fyr*."

"How long does it take?" Gundar asked.

She smiled, aware of his effort to speak with her.

"Rope for one ship can take a month," she answered.

They entered a long open shed with huge transverse rafters. "This is where we dry it," she pointed out.

The bundles were hanging from the rafters. She took down a bundle and began shaking off the seeds.

"Then over here is where we soak it." She brought him to a series of large tubs.

"We dissolve the soft parts of the plant, then the stalks are dried once more and we pull it bit by bit through the hampebraak. It breaks the stalks so we can remove the fibers from the wood. It is hard *weorc* – the men do it."

Gundar nodded.

"That fiber we pull through this hackle. Its comb separates the fibers. We do that," Eilina said.

"And then?" Gundar asked, finally joining the spirit of her teaching.

"The fibers can be spun and woven or used to make rope," she smiled, completing her lesson.

Gundar understood. Somehow, the simple truth of it all soothed him. He nodded, and smiled.

For a few moments of forgetting, Gundar was simply enjoying her company.

"Do you want to try?" she asked.

"I think not," he said.

"I think not?" she teased.

He was sure he had never met anyone like her and was not sure how to respond.

She took his hands and placed them on the hemp.

"Show him, Sigrid," she said to an old woman working there.

Sigrid began to braid the hemp strands as Gundar watched.

"Here, you try, Gundar," Eilina said, placing his hands on the braids, and then putting her hands over his on the stretched yarn.

"Take a strand in the fingers of each hand," she instructed, and began to move his hands in the rhythm of the braid.

As he felt her hand on his hands, and felt her closeness, he began to feel her not as a girl, but as a woman. Warmth moved between them.

"See?" she smiled.

Gundar suddenly pulled his hands away and stood. "No," he said, shaking his head. Then he began walking toward the cottage.

Eilina watched, wondering.

"There is another woman on his heart," Sigrid said simply. Then, seeing the disappointment on Eilina's face, added, "Let him choose. He will tell you. When he is ready."

Eilina looked to Sigrid for more.

"Give him his supper," Sigrid said, and paused to sense him. "There is darkness in him, a great anger. He is not lost, but it will be a long battle for him. The mind must heal as well as the body."

These were not words Eilina wanted to hear.

Sigrid, knowing her thoughts, said to her, "It is not for anyone of us to say why God has put this man in your path."

Eilina hesitated. "But what should I say?" Eilina asked, suddenly feeling even younger than her years.

"Empty your heart of your own desire, and listen for God's. Then words will come."

Eilina, still unsure, looked into Sigrid's face. Sigrid's strong and knowing smile comforted her, and she trusted Sigrid's words.

"Go! Go!" Sigrid said.

Eilina ran after Gundar and then turned back to shout, "Thank you, Sigrid."

* * *

When Gundar entered the cottage, Eilina was there by the *fyr*, feeding the flames so they grew bright and lively, filling the cottage with dancing light.

It was then that he saw her for the first time. He had not seen her beauty at first. No, he thought, it was not that – he had not looked at her – Helga alone had filled his vision. But now, with his body and spirit beginning to heal, he was able to see her.

She did not turn her gaze away. Her gaze was strong, her beauty and calm possessing him. The emotion confused him. Helga was the only woman he had ever known. He felt himself entering a new world, not knowing whether it was her world, or a part of his own he had never felt before.

He could see now she had a great beauty that shone from within. Her features were finely chiseled and balanced, her light brown hair long and smooth, and her green eyes clear and bright. Her smile warmed him and filled him with a calm reassuring light.

He could see under her skin the lift of fine bone circling the base of her long neck, the delicate muscles of her shoulders flowing into her delicate sloping breasts...she touched his soul as no woman ever had before. He felt warm near her. He could see new things, in new ways. He could see colors, of the clothes, the wall coverings, the rugs, emerald green, bright rusts, dark yellows. He heard the sounds of the village clearly through the windows. There were children shouting, and in the distance, the hammer of a blacksmith's anvil, the calling of crows, and nearby, the softer, sweeter sounds of the evening songbirds calling.

He wanted to speak truth to her. He said, "You should not be near me, Eilina. Shadows follow me."

"Seeds grow where it is dark," she answered.

"I do not know what is growing inside me now," he warned.

She took his hand in hers. "But where those places are, inspiration lives, if we stop fighting and bring our will under God's grace." Eilina paused before her next statement, as though considering how to say it. "Gundar," she said, "you are not alone...your wife...she thinks of you."

Gundar did not know why she said it. He had not thought of Helga for two days. It confused him now. Not because he did not love Helga, but because he thought he might never know her love again.

Then, for the first time since it had all happened he thought of someone else, someone not part of his tragedy. "You are not married," he said softly to Eilina.

"I was. Three summers ago, he went to war. Three summers, three winters, three falls, and the springs were the hardest. In the fall, word came back he had been killed," she said, thinking of the man she had loved. "He was a good man. Brave. He loved me." She looked at him kindly, half-smiling. "He was strong, and handsome, like you." She said it simply, without flattery, but it surprised him.

"You are in pain," he said.

"As everyone. We all carry it differently. If we remembered that, perhaps we would not be so unkind to each other...hold each other up a bit."

Gundar could see there were tears in her eyes, but before he could say anything, she stood, hiding her eyes with her hand. 'There is a feast tonight," she said, making an effort to be cheerful, adding, "It will be good for you." She left.

*   *   *

It was a great hall, as long as a man could throw a spear, with huge timbers holding up the roof thirty feet above them. Everywhere, the timbers were blackened or scorched by the flame and smoke of decades, a burning hearth on every wall, and a great roaring *fyr* pit in the center.

Over two hundred villagers filled the great hall with singing, dancing, cavorting, laughter, and drunkenness. The men freely kissed the women, running their hands everywhere over their bodies. Others shouted and fought, while those beside them feasted. It had been a long time since Gundar had joined such a feast.

Atop the long central table, Loki the village baker stumbled, drunk, wavering down its middle pouring one goblet after another, barely lifting the flask from one to the next, so a stream of mead poured on the table between the goblets.

"You waste the mead, Loki," his wife exclaimed.

"Nonsense," Loki answered, leaping down to reach into the hearth and pull out a flaming stick. Then, taking a mouthful of the mead and inhaling a great breath, he held the flame to his mouth to blow a stream of *fyr* all the way down the table as walked atop it once more. Everyone yelled, some jumping up while others laughed.

"He's a bastard of the *fyr*," yelled one.

"Made at one feast and born at the next!" another shouted.

Eilina held Gundar's hand, weaving through the crowd and leading him to a place at one of the great black oak plank tables. Everyone watched as they took their places. A huge leather flask was being passed around, as each of them filled their goblets with mead.

Thorald, a huge warrior at the head of the table, larger than Gundar, lifted his goblet to lead the toast.

"He is the drink leader," Eilina whispered, "everyone must keep up with him."

Gundar lifted his goblet with the others.

As each lifted his goblet, each met the eyes of the other, and then drank. Then each man and woman, as they lowered their goblets from the lips, met the eyes of another at the table, moving one by one around the table. Only then did all know it was safe to begin the feast, as when there were strangers amongst them such toasts had not always ended safely.

Slowly, as they passed around the plates of boiled meats and potatoes and began to eat, they grew at ease and exchanged a few smiles.

"Eat! Drink!" ordered Thorald.

They feasted well and it came time for celebration, dancing and music.

Eilina lead him off to a bench in front of the northern hearth where a pile of great logs was now burning softer but with still a strong glowing light.

Gundar sat with Eilina on the bench in front of the *fyr*. He looked down the hall. Across the room, men and women began dancing, casting moving shadows in the firelight on the wall. The music was loud and cheerful, but soon Gundar could not hear it.

Eilina saw he was sullen. "Every one of them has lost a child or a parent," she said.

"And still they dance?" Gundar asked.

"Life is good, Gundar, if you do not weaken," Eilina replied.

Sigrid came by and refilled their cups with mead, meeting eyes with Eilina, as though to give her courage and guidance, while Gundar turned to Eilina. "I must go in the morning."

"And when you find them, you will kill them?" Eilina asked.

The question surprised Gundar. "When I am done, I will know. When it is finished."

"And when they are all dead, will you have your answer? Will you be more?"

He watched her as she took an iron poker and separated a log from the *fyr*. The flames on the log died into glowing embers.

"Hatred is as *fyr*, Gundar," she offered, "a flame born of flame. When it burns alone, it consumes itself, and whatever holds it." She pushed the log back into the *fyr.* "When it finds hatred in others, it creates yet more hatred."

The log flared up with new flames.

"They killed my son," Gundar said.

"And have you killed any man's son? Any man's father?" she asked.

"In battle. With honor," Gundar said, defending his actions.

Eilina shook her head. "Do you think their sons or fathers now care how their loved ones were lost to them?"

He hesitated, saying simply, "It is my world."

"Where vengeance makes right?" Eilina asked.

She laid her soft palm to his face. "There is another way. Seek it out. Do not fight it when it comes. It will save you. It is the only thing that will save you. Hate cannot return lost love, Gundar. Only you can give that back to yourself."

Their eyes met and he knew she was trying to tell him something he could not understand. Not because he did not want to, but because he had never heard such things before.

"Tomorrow, I leave, to find my daughter," he said.

"You must speak with our priest, Gundar," Eilina pleaded. "Magni will help you. Speak with him."

"I could worship any god or demon that might help me," he said, "but they do not listen. We are only their play things."

Eilina was silent for a moment. "There are other worlds, where we are not." She stood, kissed him on the cheek, and left.

He looked at the log she had pushed back into the *fyr*. The flames were engulfing it, as the sounds of the feasting and revelry rushed back in upon him. 'What worlds,' he wondered.

* * *

When he entered her cottage, it was warm. The *fyr* was burning brightly. Yet something was different. He could feel it, or maybe it was because now he knew he was leaving. He saw the life she had made there, the implements of cooking, her small loom, threaded with reds and greens. It was a good home and a warm one. And he felt her love here.

He moved toward her room with a sense of anticipation, as though knowing what to expect. Something had changed within him these past few days. He remembered once when after months at sea he had taken that first breath that smelled of land, telling him that he had made it home. It was that comfort and that quiet strength that he felt now, so for this single moment he did not think of Thor, or Helga, or Lina. He only held them in his heart, without fear. Eilina's love lit in him the flame of a new hope, a light that might sustain him on the journey ahead.

Because, just now, he could see. She had made him see, or feel. He could see all that he could not see before. What lay ahead was not what had gone before. All these new horizons, mingling within him like the swirling lighted mists of sunrise, made landscapes he had never before seen or imagined.

What did she want of him? What did she know of him? He pushed open the door to her room. If he listened to her, if he went her way, he could be with her, would be with her now – but would he be with himself? He knew he wanted both.

She was there, as he knew she would be, waiting on the bed, atop the furs, naked, honest, without modesty.

Her smooth milk-colored skin highlighted the rose of her erect nipples. Her breathing lifted her breasts up and down as she waited silently. He watched her breasts fall into her flat belly and the smooth triangle between her thighs. He could feel his heart beating and his blood rising in his loins as he approached her with slow and uncertain steps. When he was only a few feet from her, he hesitated, turning partly back toward the door.

Time stood still, as she waited and he stood, one side to her bed, the other to the door. She waited without asking. His desire now was new, unknown to him. She did not look toward him or beckon him. He knew she wanted his choice to be his own.

He stepped toward the bed and kneeled down beside her. Everything else in his life vanished. He placed his hand upon her, caressing toward her lower belly. He looked into her eyes, and she finally met his, still waiting, patiently, for what he would choose.

"You have a great beauty, Eilina," he said.

When he said it, they both knew. It was in his voice.

In that moment, their friendship was sealed and their love lost. Or it would be a different kind of love.

But he knew there would be sorrow for her, as there was for him, in a different way.

Still holding her gaze, he slowly pulled the robe back over her. She expected it, but she put her hand over his as he did it.

Eilina had no words. She knew she would never meet another man like Gundar. She knew she would never feel for another man what she felt for him.

For a long moment, they breathed in the silence between them, until Gundar gave her the only thing he could give her now.

"I will go to the priest in the morning, before I leave."

Eilina smiled and tears came from her eyes, glad that he would seek the wisdom as she had asked, and sad that he would be leaving.

He leaned over and kissed her on the lips, not quietly, but with a soft passion, letting her know he knew she was a woman. She met his kiss, lifting up her chest to him, and then their kiss grew and began to fill them, until they both stopped, somehow both knowing when to stop.

Gundar caressed her hair. "I have not enough words to thank you —"

She put her finger upon his lips, "It all we ever really have...what we give to others..." she said.

Gundar nodded, and stood.

"I won't forget you." He held her gaze a moment longer before leaving her.

*　*　*

At dawn, with the sun still behind the mountains, Gundar found himself walking down a path in a light rain toward a small wooden stave church.

When he was still far away, he saw the priest pulling down dead animals that hung from poles around the church. He threw first the animals, mostly foxes and hares, and then the poles, into the tall grass far away from the church.

"Pagans!" he shouted loudly enough for Gundar to hear, and then, seeing Gundar approaching, disappeared into the church.

Gundar entered cautiously, underneath a dragon carved above the door. It was churches such as these that he had often entered as a raider.

The rising sun sent colored rays through the stained glass windows. He began walking down the aisle between the six rough-hewn benches on each side. There were images in the windows he had never seen, except for one. It was the hooded face of a beautiful woman. He had seen it on the scrolls.

"Your sweords, Gundar," a voice said from the front of the church.

"I have none," Gundar answered the voice.

Gundar felt a not unfamiliar presence in the room. It was the power he had felt when he first felt the scrolls. He walked down the aisle toward the altar. He found the priest, Magni, to one side of the altar, polishing a silver chalice with a small piece of fleece.

"I came only because of a promise," Gundar stated.

"Grace like candlelight flickers in the wind of doubt, Gundar. You believe God has betrayed you,"

Magni said, "like all men, when their life is not made according to their own will."

Gundar, surprised by the priest's bold tone, answered just as boldly. "Or betrayed as the old men of the village without hands or feet."

"Men act in ignorance claiming right," Magni offered, "serving the gods of their imagination. With all the dreams, and all the hopes of all the races through all the ages, you will not touch God, or see him, or speak with Him."

"What god is that?" Gundar wanted to know.

"The one God, who would save us from our pride and ignorance, from all that separates us from the rest of God's creatures. We must put our soul into God's keeping, to whom it is much wiser to entrust than ourselves, so we might come into Grace, which is always waiting for us."

"I am certain it waits for me no longer," Gundar replied.

Magni finished polishing the chalice and placed in on the stone altar. He looked over his shoulder at Gundar, knowing it was just plunder to him, and then continued speaking. "Grace is not something we find or even ask for. It's a blessing we receive when we know who we truly are, not in the eyes of others, but in the eyes of God."

"I had a son," Gundar said. "He was murdered."

"As did the one God, a son, crucified by the Romans a thousand years ago that the world might understand love, among all men."

Gundar placed his scrolls before Magni. "Can you speak these marks?"

Magni took them into their hands with reverence. When he opened the first one, Gundar saw his face change. "It's not possible," he said aloud to himself. He began reading, astonished, and tears came into his eyes.

"What is it?" Gundar asked. "What do they speak?"

Magni slowly looked up, looking into Gundar's eyes, wondering why it was that Gundar had been so chosen, to hold these sacred scrolls.

"It is the Gospel of John," Magni said, "the most devoted disciple of Christ, God's son."

"Can it bring back my son from the dead?" Gundar asked.

Magni, seeing Gundar's pain, tried to answer with compassion.

"No, but it can bring <u>you</u> to him," Magni said. "Life is an unraveling, Gundar, the life we hoped to live and did not live, the life before us that seeks our courage, and the life in God, which extends from birth to death, and burns, when grace or will ignites, in single moments of eternity. That is the life in Christ. That is where you will find your son."

"My eyes have seen the *weorcs* of this Christ," Gundar said.

"No. Of those who *weorc* in his name. The animal in man takes all things to its own purpose. So before he was killed, the son of God left a Spirit to guide men that they would not be alone, the Spirit to know what is true, for when love of truth is among men this Spirit will be there, too, and when this Spirit abides amongst them they will know truth when it is spoken," Magni said. "You think you can find life by taking it away? That your hate will give you back what you have

141

lost? How can a shadow become light? Only by the light of Grace."

"The marks, priest. Tell me what they say," Gundar persisted.

Magni, seeing Gundar was not understanding, gave him other words he hoped Gundar could hear.

"I have told you," Magni said, "Vengeance is mine, I will repay, says this God."

Gundar heard him, and felt, for a moment his rage cooling toward a terrible sadness. But he stopped himself, fearing it would weaken his will.

Magni saw it, and touched Gundar on the shoulder. "It is a different strength that lies on the far shore of that sea. I pray one day you will set sail there, and step onto that shore."

Suddenly Magni turned his head, hearing something.

"Free yourself, Gundar," Magni said and disappeared through a heavy wooden door into the back of the church.

Gundar quickly rolled the scrolls and placed them in his pouch. Now he could hear it too, the sound of marching. He suddenly realized he was unarmed. He looked around for any weapon, or anything he could use as a weapon. On the wall nearby was a heavy iron crucifix. He yanked it from the wall and stood just behind the door, ready to strike anyone who entered.

The marching grew louder and he heard voices.

"If he is still here we will find him," said the first.

"Remember, he is to live," answered the second.

Gundar knew they were speaking of him, but why let him live? They wanted something from him. The scrolls?

The marching warriors passed in front of the church. Gundar stood silently, his back against the wall. He tried to listen to their footsteps to hear how many men were there. Over thirty, he guessed. But then the marching faded as they passed.

He waited another moment and then slipped out the door, staying close to the church, and looking in either direction. The sun had vanished and the sky was growing darker.

He slipped alongside to the path through the trees, making his way toward Eilina's cottage.

* * *

As Goth arrived at the village with his men, he smiled to himself. The thunder rumbling over the distant mountains seemed a good omen. He turned his head toward the sky to taste the rain, and then laughed. Perhaps it was time to kill Gundar after all.

"Bring them! All of them!" he roared to his men.

His men disappeared in all directions to bring the villagers to the village center. Old men, women, children, and the men not working in the fields were all assembled before Goth.

"We are looking for a man!" Goth yelled.

The headman stepped forward. "We have no strangers here."

"We will see," Goth said, motioning them in closer with a wave.

Goths warriors began pushing all the villagers directly before him, so he towered over them.

"We seek the outlaw, Gundar," Goth roared.

When no one answered, he drew his sweord, "If your memories are short we can make other parts short as well."

"Enough. He is no outlaw," Eilina said to stop him from making further threats.

Two warriors rushed to Eilina, and dragged her to Goth, throwing her down on the ground before him.

One of Goth's men whispered in his ear.

Goth said, "He is wise to take comfort where he can find it."

Eilina looked up to him calmly and without fear. "As such a man deserves," she said.

Goth saw her courage and was impressed, but demanded, "Tell me where he has gone."

"He seeks a man," Eilina answered.

"What man?" Goth asked, suspicious of her tone.

Eilina began to stand, but the warriors held down her shoulders.

Goth notched his head upward, and they let her stand. She looked up to Goth, who towered over her, and met his eyes.

"The man who seeks him," she answered.

Goth, infuriated, drew his sword and stepped closer to her, asking, "You play with me?"

Eilina made the sign of the cross on her forehead and kneeled back down.

"Speak!" Goth roared.

She reached into a pocket and withdrew a small silver cross on a neck chain. "He left this for you."

Goth looked down at the cross in her hand and knew she was lying.

He looked into her eyes and saw no apology for her lie but bold defiance in the face of his disbelief. Why? But the cross held some power over him, and he stepped back.

"Take her back to her hut," Goth ordered.

Aslak stood nearby, leering at her. "I will take her."

He grabbed Eilina by the arm and began walking away.

Eilina, sensing his intentions, struggled to pull away.

"No," she cried, but Aslak had her firmly in his grip as he began dragging her toward a nearby cottage.

"Search the village. Harm no one," Goth commanded.

* * *

Gundar entered Eilina's cottage.

"Eilina," he whispered, but she was not there. He quickly tied his folded scrolls to his belly under his tunic and grabbed his broken sweord from its wrapping, tying a rag tightly around the bottom of the upper half. He then slung his quiver over his back and his bow around his shoulder.

As Gundar emerged from the cottage, he saw a line of warriors on the field's edge. He would have to cut through their line near the far end, and then break into the woods. He slipped from one cottage to the next, drawing closer.

145

Then, drawing the two sweord halves in each hand, one by the hilt, one by the blade, he rushed the line. Before a single cry went out, he was upon them. Slashing downward and out, he slashed the chests of the two men between him and safety.

But two other warriors who had seen him coming still stood their ground behind the line. The first warrior swung sideways at his head. Diving to the ground, he ducked the blow, and rolling back to his feet thrust upward into his stomach with his sweordpoint. The other warrior's sweord struck his arm a glancing blow off his arm guard. He pivoted around to slash him across the chest and then swing overhead down through his helmet into his head. His path was clear to break free and run into the forest. Then he heard a scream. Eilina! Seeing a dozen warriors turning toward him, he raced into the trees, running with all his speed. Once he was certain they could no longer see him, he turned suddenly, making a great circle back toward the huts.

* * *

Aslak grabbed Eilina by the hair and dragged her into her cottage, throwing her down on the ground.

She stared back at him with fiery resolve. "You will fail," she said.

He climbed over her.

She pushed against him with both arms with all her force as he pushed his knee into her thigh to open her legs. When she tried to turn on her side to stop him, he slapped her back and forth across her face and shook her.

"You bitch!" he yelled.

She grabbed a stick from near the hearth and struck him across the face, drawing blood.

Enraged, he made a fist to strike her.

Sixty yards away, Gundar burst from the forest, his eyes on the window of Eilina's cottage. As two warriors rushed him, Gundar whipped his bow over his shoulder, notching and pulling an arrow to fire it between them.

"You whore!" Aslak yelled at Eilina, raising his fist above his head to strike her.

Gundar's arrow flew through the window to burst through Aslak's chest. Eilina gasped as he fell dead over her. She pushed him off and struggled to stand.

Gundar slew the two attacking warriors to reach Eilina's cottage as she stumbled out of it. The shouting of the men he had left behind in the forest grew closer.

Eilina was shaking. He put her arm over his shoulder, and held her around the waist to support her.

"Come on," he said, supporting her and hurrying her toward the village smithy where he had seen two horses.

"Go, Gundar, they'll kill you," Eilina said.

Gundar ignored her warning as he watched for danger around them, wanting only to protect her.

When they arrived at the smithy, there was only one horse, saddled. He threw Eilina up on it.

"Ride south to Innisgard. Ask for Skuli."

"Gundar, no," Eilina protested, "You must take it. Please."

Gundar struck the horse hard on the hindquarters, yelling, "Yaah!" and took off running, looking over his shoulder to see two warriors racing toward him near the tree line. He drew his bow, but they stopped short, still fifty yards away.

He took a last glance at Eilina vanishing down the path, and then turned and raced sideways across the field's edge back into the forest.

CHAPTER ELEVEN

A GREATER SWEORD

He had outpaced his pursuers, but he knew he could not travel without a weapon. Even his fierce will could not save him with only his knife. He had to think of something. He waited until he came upon a stream.

He searched the streambed for a square stone, lifting and feeling the weight of one after another. When he found one he liked, he threw it hard against another rock. It shattered. He found another one, threw it. When he examined it, it was chipped. He kept looking. Finally, he found another, hard, shiny and black. When he threw it down, it shattered everything it hit.

Within the saplings on the hillside above the stream, he looked for a shaft. He put his fist around one tree after another until he found the right fit. He felled the sapling, and then cut it to length with his knife, and stripped the bark. He swung it back and forth through the air to test its balance. When he was satisfied it would serve his purpose, he drew another piece of sinew from inside his tunic.

As he looked at it, a thought crossed his mind. He realized, even now, Helga was helping him – he remembered she had wisely sewn two pockets inside his tunic. Here he kept his few valuable possessions for his journey. Whatever her feelings now, he took some encouragement from the thought.

He began to carefully bind the stone to the shaft to make a great hammer. When it was complete, he swung it overhead and down upon a great boulder, smashing it into the pieces. The binding held. He threw the hammer's shaft over his shoulder and found the trail again to continue on his way.

His stride was a little stronger, and his will fierce again. So the fearsome god Thor had his hammer – now he had his.

After a couple of hours, he found a smaller trail leading off toward the base of the gray cliffs. He sensed this was the path he was seeking, and turned off to climb the trail up the hillside.

Suddenly, as he climbed, a broad-chested dwarfed man in full armor leapt in front of him, holding a great gleaming battle-axe across his chest.

"Our land!" he growled, confronting Gundar, although only slightly more than half his height.

In seconds, the first man was joined by a second, then a third, and then more, until there were five like him, all with battle axes, all fully armored, surrounding him in a half circle.

Gundar beheld them, astonished by their bright and finely crafted silver armor. Silver belts and armguards, scrolled breastplates, helmets trimmed with gold, and the finest chain mail he had ever seen shone brightly in his eyes. Then it was true, what they said about these dwarfed men of the mountains. They were masters of the metal craft. He had come to the right place.

With a mighty sideways swing, Gundar launched his stone axe over the trees far below, and held up a hand in peace. "I seek Vindalf."

"Who seeks him?" Thrain, the eldest man asked.

Gundar walked into their midst without fear, as they backed away, lifting their axes before their chests.

"Gundar, son of Avangar."

There was a murmur of recognition amongst them. "Avangar..."

The men lowered their axes as Thrain stepped forward. "Vindalf has gone down to the river," he said, adding, "If you come for a sweord, then come with us."

Suddenly the rushing of arrows filled the air, and the dull thud of arrowheads striking flesh. As Gundar spun around drawing his sweord to face the attack, more arrows struck the men all around him, dropping them all to the ground. Hooves clattered and spun as only the dim shapes of the mounted attackers were visible through the trees and dust as they vanished with the sound of hooves thundering and then fading into the mountainside.

Then all was silent. Gundar looked around. He kneeled down beside each man, checking for signs of life with his hand against each throat. There was no movement, no breath, not a groan. He looked at the face of the last one. They were all dead. Only he had been left standing.

Suddenly behind him, he heard heavy footsteps racing up the hill. Vindalf appeared, axe in one hand, and a wooden box under one arm. He stopped, seeing Gundar kneeling down beside one of his hearth-companions. Gundar stood and put his hand to his knife, but Vindalf saw that Gundar's bow still hung on his back, and he had heard the horses rush past as they left.

Vindalf threw down his battleaxe. He went to one of the fallen men and kneeled down beside him, placing his box down beside him. Seeing he was dead, he grasped the silver cross around his neck, and broke the chain to grab it off. He opened the box and put it in.

He said to Gundar, "My brother, Althjof. He believed in the new religion."

Gundar nodded, not knowing why that mattered now.

More than a dozen armed men suddenly rushed forward from the mouth of the cave. Some took up positions as the cave's mouth while other tended to the dead.

Vindalf folded his dead brother's hands over his chest and put a hand over his brother's crossed hands. For a moment, he was silent as though making a vow. Then he rose as his hand formed into a fist.

"They hunt us and kill us like animals, King Olaf's men. We are not welcome in his new world," Vindalf said.

He stood, picking up his box, and walked past Gundar. "Follow me," Vindalf said as he passed, and disappeared into the cave.

Gundar surveyed the scene he was leaving, and the cave entrance ahead, and then followed. A long torch-lined hall lay ahead.

Vindalf took one of the torches off the wall of the cave and descended down a long tunnel into the mountains, crossing through the darkness that lay between one torch and the next.

Gundar, walking behind him, soon could hear the steady dull hammering and sharp striking of many smiths at anvils and forge. The cave began to grow unevenly brighter in scattered light and shadow from distant flames.

At last, they reached a giant cavern, filled with many fires whose smoke vanished into crevices overhead. The cavern was as large as any great timber hall he had ever seen. Three men worked on anvils, two more at a dozen fiery forges that lit the cavern with a deep red glow. All were dwarfed. Others moved supplies from one working station to another. Several looked at him as he passed, but he walked on as though not noticing.

Vindalf stood waiting in front of small grotto in the rear of the cavern. He waved Gundar over to him.

"Our race has learned many secrets. Paid gold for knowledge from the far ends of the world." He studied Gundar for a long moment. "You come for a sweord. Many have come. So I ask, is it to kill or to protect?"

Vindalf waited, but Gundar had no answer.

"No man has ever had an answer. Maybe you will be the first to find one."

Vindalf turned his back and reached up to a high shelf cut into the rock wall. He drew down a long finely made and polished wooden box with silver hinges, placing it on the table before Gundar.

"We do not give our deepest knowledge to men, nor use it in the sweords we sell to them," he pronounced.

Vindalf opened the box to reveal a magnificent sweord with an intricately carved golden hilt and finely etched blade.

"Once each generation, to preserve our knowledge and our craft, we make two sweords. One to keep, one to *weorc*." He held the blade across his open palms, offering it to Gundar. "My brother gave his every hour night and day for many months to craft it."

Gundar took the sweord, turning it in the light as he examined it. In all his life, and all his travels, he had never seen such a fine sweord as what he now held in his hand. He turned its gleaming blade round and back in the light of the fires.

"He prayed over it, that it might guide its bearer in the Holy Spirit. It is for you if you will have it, and make its *weorc* yours," Vindalf said.

Gundar put the sweord back into Vindalf's hands. "I have not the gold for as great a sweord as this," Gundar said.

"We fought beside your father, Gundar. Your story travels to us through the hills and the forests. We know your troubles. Now, I know mine. But do not be alone in your quest, Gundar," he said, "living in the world of your enemy. Do not make his mind yours, or isolate yourself from those that would help you."

Gundar was beginning to understand.

"By itself, it cannot avenge my brother," Vindalf said, laying the sweord back in his hands.

Gundar took the sweord and holding it upward, ran the edge of his left hand along it.

He met Vindalf's eyes, and nodded. "Then by my will, it shall," he vowed.

Vindalf nodded back, holding Gundar's gaze, so in the coming battle their sorrows might be joined.

"Goth is the man you seek," Vindalf spoke. "Son of Aleric…"

Recognition and memory awoke in Gundar. "Goth…"

CHAPTER TWELVE
THE ICE CROSSING

Gundar walked out of the forest onto a vast frozen plain that glared white in his eyes, into the valley of the ice lakes. On the ice blue horizon, ten miles distant, he saw the rocky snow-covered mountains with great granite peaks and walls rising into the heavens from where descended great white rivers of ice.

He kicked at the snow and ice at his feet. It swirled upward and vanished into the strong wind. It would be a hard passage that he might not survive. He steeled himself with thoughts of Helga and his daughter. At his feet, the first frozen lake stood in his path.

He looked up and down the valley. Everywhere, there were more frozen lakes, like a hundred icebound shields. He looked up to the surrounding snow-covered mountains rising up to meet the ceramic blue sky, where the white winter sun was rising in the northeast. To walk around the valley floor would take five days or more. He would have to cross it.

Across on the far side of the valley, he thought he could see a path cutting through the place where two ridges fell into one another and water flowed from the boulder-strewn mouth of a retreating glacier.

He would have to make it to the other side before nightfall.

From the sky, scattered snowflakes were falling. Already the light was dimming and he knew the snow would soon fall harder.

He walked the few step down to the lake and began his march, lifting his steps over the deepening snow. The wind and falling snow blew hard against him, making every two of his steps only count as one. He could not see ahead of himself more than a few feet, so

159

he kept his head down, laboring against the blowing wind. The hours passed as his strength grew less. When he reached the center, ice began cracking under his feet. He stopped, thinking the ice supporting him might be growing thinner. He began testing his steps, and realized it was only surface ice forming atop the hard lake ice. He marched on, at last reaching the far frozen shore.

Without stopping, he pushed on toward the second lake. The snow between the lakes reached up to his knees. The wind grew colder and fiercer, driving toward his bones. He began his crossing of the second lake.

Somehow, he found himself thinking of Aleric, the chieftain he had slain, the man who was Goth's father.

He remembered looking into his eyes when he thrust his sweord into his belly. He had felt Aleric's spirit leave his body, felt his soul touch his before departing.

'I taught you well, Gundar,' Aleric had said as he collapsed to his knees. 'Your sweord is strong, but be wise and do not follow it.'

Such were these wars and these times, village fighting against village, and family against family. Yet he knew now it had been the beginning of his sorrows, the beginning of this new war.

He was freezing and exhausted. He did not want to think now, but everything counted now, to save his daughter. From what fate? Who was Goth? What man had he become, this boy he had once known?

He tried to remember that boy, always by far the biggest, the strongest – yet he had never taken advantage, would spar only with the grown men of the village. How now had he come by such hate? How could it have grown so within him? If he was owed a debt for his father's death, why did he not try to settle it at the Wergild time? All those years he had never asked the judges for restitution, for the customary twelve cows for a chieftain, or a parcel of land – Goth's anger was beyond the just laws of their villages, or any village.

And for this now, Goth's hate grew. And for this now, Gundar knew the hate grew in him, too.

By mid-afternoon he had had crossed the second lake, and was walking the mile of flat land before the last and final lake. The snow had stopped and the sun was growing low in the sky. At first, there was new snow on the ground but then the surface grew icier. He knew now he could not turn back. His feet began to grow numb. The wind sliced against his neck, his footsteps crushing the hard snow underfoot like the gravel of a streambed. He set out over the third lake.

After two hours, the snow under his feet grew harder, finally turning to ice. His feet began to slip. He had left the lakeshore far behind and could not turn back. He had to reach the forested hills ahead. The sky cleared. But after another hour, with his feet slipping underneath him, he realized he would not make it across the lake before night fell.

The icy wind was growing stronger, striking his neck and chest like fierce knives as the far horizon exploded into a molten crimson seam between snow and sky. His freezing limbs were growing sluggish and his blood cold, and his death seemed as near as the wind on his uncovered throat.

He lifted his head to the heavens and raised his arms into the sky, roaring like a trapped animal. The cold would not have him. He would not let it. He surveyed the ice beneath his feet, as far as his eyes could see.

To the north, he saw the tops of reeds pushing through the ice. It was the only life for miles around. Instinctively, he turned toward them and began to walk until he was amongst them. He stopped and heard his own hoarse breath, in and out of his throat. He knew his next decision would be his last – live or die.

As the sun began to set, he took his knife and began feverishly to cut the tops of reeds protruding through the ice. At first, his knife sliced through the tough stalks, until they began to dull his blade. Then he had to saw though them, consuming precious time, time he did not have.

The reeds stood in clumps of only two to three, forcing him to make thirty or forty steps to gather each full handful. He threw each handful into a pile making a circle of piles as he moved. The wind blew harder, driving into his muscles with a biting chill, slowing them. The red sun was touching the flat ice horizon. When darkness came, if he was not sheltered, he would be dead. Staying bent down, he cut more and more reeds, looking up again and again to check the sun's descent.

Finally, with the sweat freezing into a mask on his face, he gathered up all the piles into his arms and laid them down together on the ice. Then, kneeling down and holding them against the wind, he pulled out a long string of sinew from his tunic pocket. A fierce gust stole away a handful of reeds as he grabbed the remaining reeds closer. Biting one end of the sinew, he twisted the reeds upright into a crude spiraling structure. He fumbled with numb fingers trying to tie the knots around them two-thirds up their length. The sinew slipped to the ground. He grabbed for it before the wind carried it away. Finally, he succeeded in tying the reds together. The remaining reeds he threw onto the ice to make a crude floor.

With the wind fighting against him, he climbed inside and curled up on his knees and elbows, trying to hold some warmth against the freezing air. He pulled the scrolls from his tunic, carefully placing them where he could not crush them. Even the darkness inside his crude shelter he welcomed now, if it could provide the least warmth against the cold stars.

Time slowed. Through the mists of exhaustion and half-sleep, he was fading in and out of consciousness, shivering through the longest hours he had ever known. Dreams of Helga were becoming sad nightmares, reminding him of his loss, of Thor. He wished the ice would reach into his heart to still his pain.

Two hours before dawn the wind grew fiercer, howling and whistling in violent gusts. The wind began to blow and bend the reeds, finally breaking the sinew. His crude shelter began to tear apart. He tried to hold it together, and failed.

Then, before he could grab them, the scrolls blew from his scattering shelter, vanishing in swirling white winds across the lake. For a long moment, he stared after them through the strands of his ice-covered hair, wondering what he might have lost forever.

* * *

Skuli had told her to make her way north, quietly, that he would bring Gundar to the coast with their daughter. Helga had no other choice but to trust him, and to hope. She had been hiking for weeks, eating the herbs and fruit she could find along the way. At villages, she used the silver coins Skuli had given her to buy bread and dried meat. Her clothes were worn and dirty, and she had folded the tresses of her long blond hair under a leather helmet.

This morning she had been hiking since dawn. Her feet now were open blisters, and her legs more weary than she had ever known. It was not midday yet, but she had to stop and rest.

Coming upon a stream, she knelt down beside a small circling pool and began washing the sweat and grime off her face. When she was done, her reflection began to appear in the calming water. She did not like what she saw. It was the face of a woman grown hard, hard but not bitter, not yet.

She gazed at the reflection as though looking into her own life…in the spring, when the meadow was filled with the colors of wildflowers, she was walking hand in hand with Lina and Thor, Gundar walking alongside, the warmth of the sun on their faces. A current disturbed the pool, and the memory of her love and happiness, like her own image, vanished.

With a cupped hand, she lifted the water to her lips. The taste was sweet, and she drank more, trying to forget.

Still, the sorrow came. It came over her like a great wave, and for the first time since she had been a small child, she could not keep herself from crying. It was a sorrow greater than her strength, greater than

164

any hope of persevering. Her fierce will dissolved as rock into sand beneath the ocean's pounding, and she wailed for her lost family, in great sobs that took away her breath and shook her chest.

When it was over, and she could cry no more, she felt her body unmoving, as though her blood pulsed and her breath moved without her, as the sounds of the forest returned. The stream was pouring, and the branches brushed against one another in the wind. The birds and small animals, lemmings, grebes, and hazel grouse, moved around her, on the ground, and in the trees. For a long time, she listened, alone with the sounds.

Then she drew a deep breath, and stood. The sun was glinting though the tree branches now, low in the sky. Her anger was slipping away from her, and she could not hold it.

She thought of Gundar, and knew that she would never love any other man.

* * *

Hours before dawn, the wind was still blowing great sheets of snow and sleet across the lakes. Gundar leaned into the fierce gusts, fighting for each step and every foot of ground. The far shore was drifting in and out of his vision, as his fingers turned blue and his lungs burned in the cold. He put his hands under his arms trying to keep them warm, still trying to keep his balance. He slipped, and fell hard, face forward. He tried to get up, but collapsed again.

He pulled out a dagger, stabbing into the ice. The point chipped the ice but did not penetrate it. He stabbed again, and it held, allowing him to pull himself along yard by yard. His muscles began to burn, and then fail.

He could no longer see the shore when his arms finally gave out. He put his head down against the wind, searching for some greater will that would renew his strength, but found none.

Through the snow, he saw an image of Helga. The image was fading in and out. Its edges were clear and then hazy. Her eyes came, and then her face. Her expression haunted him because there was none.

"Helga! Helga!" he called out into the vast frozen wilderness, but there was no answer, only the fierce rushing of the cold wind and snow now engulfing him.

CHAPTER THIRTEEN

ALL OUR CHILDREN

"Leave me!" cried Goth, waving his men out of his lodge.

He was sharpening his sweord with a black stone before the hearth. His timber lodge was dark and quiet except for the light of the flames, and the whispering logs. He worked to make his sweord perfect like his revenge.

But as he looked at Lina, huddling small and frail in the corner, memories came to him. He turned his gaze back into the flames.

...in his mother's house, the rays of sunlight entered the room without brightening it, as though unable to dispel his dark and heavy thought.

His mother was there, quietly going about her preparations, laying her clothes and her jewelry into wooden trunks.

Goth was desperate to speak, but did not know how to begin.

'Why?' he was saying. 'Why?! What if there are no other worlds?!'

'I go my way, Goth,' she answered, continuing her *weorc*.

He paced nervously behind her, finally turning to her. 'It is not enough that he's gone? Is it a voyage to the next village, mother?'

'It is not so different,' she answered quietly, 'and I have been done no harm,' she said.

'No harm?! Your husband is killed!' Goth protested.

'With honor, he goes to Valhalla. I thank the warrior that sends him to take his place there.'

'It is the old way,' Goth protested. 'This is what my father wanted!' Goth protested, holding up a silver chain and cross. 'He was going to leave the old gods!'

His mother stopped 'What is it, my son? Is it that we leave you alone with no brother or sister?' she asked, laying the palm of her hand softly on his face.

Goth turned his face, pulling away.

...the image faded into the flames, and he saw his mother being lifted within a crowd, still standing, by two strong young warriors, reciting the ancient chant...

'Lo, there do my eyes behold my father and my mother,

Lo, there do my eyes behold my sisters and my brothers...'

He remembered fighting the sorrow that rose in his chest, fighting it until it became something else, something he could control, the hate that had now become his life.

He turned back at Lina and looked at her. She met his gaze as though feeling his thoughts and the danger approaching her. He wanted to make her part of that hate, but he knew she was only a child.

He was not ready to give the order to throw her from the cliffs. Not yet.

He walked to the great timber door and pulled across the giant cross latch, high above Lina's reach.

He looked over to her. "Sleep," he said, throwing her a fur robe, and retiring to his bed.

* * *

Goth awoke, and still groggy, half-stumbled outside to relief himself. As he did, he looked back up over the rising steam of his water at his fine timber lodge amidst the tall trees of this northern forest, and was pleased with himself, and his accomplishments. It had taken a hundred of his men two years to build. There was not a finer lodge for three hundred miles around.

As he turned round, suddenly thirty warriors, surrounding him with spears and sweords drawn, rushed him. Not knowing fear, he reached for his sweord. Only when he saw more coming did he take his hand from its hilt.

"Goth, I should have known you were the wild bear in the middle of this trouble," said a huge warrior, Valgard Blood-axe, almost as big as Goth, as he emerged through the field of spears.

"Olaf forgets his old hearth-companions and sends a boy to do his bidding," Goth said.

"We come for the traitor's daughter," Valgard said. "Now! Her!"

Valgard was pointing through the door at Lina, who was peering out around its edge. "Take her!" he ordered.

Goth looked around, and decided to say nothing. Still, four warriors put their spears toward Goth's throat.

"She is nothing to me," Goth said.

"His family will die with his name and bloodline. Come dawn we will throw this one from traitor's cliff on Trollveggen," Valgard said.

Goth wondered if it was the gods' decree that the decision whether to kill or spare Lina be taken from him.

Valgard nodded to his men and they withdrew their spears as two other warriors began to lead Lina off.

Lina looked to Goth, now her last contact with any known world or safety.

Goth saw her longing looks, but then laughed as the warriors carried her off, "She's your trouble now."

The warriors laughed with him, but Valgard looked at him closely, not trusting his words. Goth noticed it, but ignored him.

Lina took the moment's distraction to break free of her captor's hold and run. She had only made it a few feet before another warrior grabbed her, lifting her into the air so her feet could not touch the ground.

Goth, seemingly thinking nothing more of Lina, shouted, "Mead will finish our *weorc* today!"

The other warriors roared in approval and sheathed their sweords.

"And meat," one of them yelled.

"Meat and mead," another yelled. "A boar to roast!"

"A boar it will be! Iuli!" Goth shouted to a man outside the great lodge. "A feast for the king's men!"

Iuli waved back with a closed fist, as though acknowledging some secret command.

An hour later, most of Valgard's warriors, already full of mead and good spirit, were joining Goth in his lodge.

As all lifted their glasses to toast, Valgard met the eyes of each of Goth's warriors, but suddenly saw Goth

172

was standing back from the table. He saw, too, there were too many servants standing behind them, more than Goth could possibly have. It was too late.

The servants were warriors who had exchanged their clothes with Goth's servants, who were the ones now seated at the feast. Goth's warriors withdrew their long knives and pulled back the heads of thirty of Valgard's men to slash their throats as they sat.

Four archers rushed into the room and shot Valgard through the stomach and chest.

He threw his goblet at Goth and yelled, "A traitor's death you will get from King Olaf!"

As Valgard fell to his knees, Goth pushed him over with his foot, declaring, "I know no king by that name," as he stepped over him, and dropped his half-eaten boar's leg on Valgard's dead body.

"Olaf will have your head on a pike," Blokr said.

"If he can afford to lose any more men," Goth scoffed, and turned to his men to roar, "Come on now! We'll finish the *bloodweorc*!"

The warriors rushed from the lodge, grabbing sweords and spears as they exited.

As Goth's men fought with King Olaf's warriors, Goth slipped out the back of the lodge and rushed to the cliffs of Trollveggen.

* * *

CHAPTER FOURTEEN

A FACE IN THE WIND

When Gundar became conscious, he was being dragged across the ice through the blowing snowfall. He could feel his body being pulled, step-by-step, a foot at a time, toward the lakeshore.

With each step, he heard muttering. "Hard to find as the white bear...thank Odin you were calling her name...or you'd be dead for sure." Then he was dragged a few more steps, and the rescuer gasped, "Only the likes of you would think to follow its way here." Then he stopped for a couple of deep breaths, before pulling him along again. "Your fur may not be so thick," giving him a hard yank, and complaining, "but I am sure you weigh as much."

But Gundar heard nothing more. He had lapsed back into unconsciousness.

He half-awoke to the cries of a flock of gannets flying overhead. He was lying beside a *fyr* under a rock ledge, covered with a fur. His eyes tried to open to the dawn, but he fell back into troubled dreams that turned and twisted as the strands of a braided rope...until the thrashing of branches and approaching footsteps startled him.

He propped himself up on an elbow, straining to see into the falling snow, reaching around on the ground for his sweord. A shape was approaching, knocking the snow from the branches.

He yelled at it, "Hold! Are you of this world or another?"

"If not this one, then I have spent thirty years in the wrong place!" the voice answered.

"Skuli!" Gundar was startled to see Skuli's smiling face emerging from the mist, and his arms full of

177

broken branches and long saplings. Gundar was sure had never seen a more welcome sight.

Skuli sat down beside the *fyr* and began feeding the branches to the flames. "A hundred masts Skuli drags you across the ice, thinking Gundar follows the path of the white bear."

Gundar half-smiled and felt the growing flames begin to warm him.

Skuli looked up, adding, "His fur is not so thick, but I am sure he weighs as much!"

Gundar warmed, too, to Skuli's bright spirit. "I thank the gods that have sent you, Skuli."

"Skuli sends Skuli. Leaving me to grow old and feeble in my cottage, while your adventures bring glory to your name! You may forget Skuli, but Skuli does not forget you!"

"Adventures?" Gundar said, shaking his head. "No, only troubles."

"Some good trouble is what I sorely need!" Skuli complained.

Gundar half-laughed, for the first time since his tragedy. "Then I will share with you – what is mine is yours, my friend," he said, feeling the bond of life with the man who was his closest hearth-companion.

"How in Odin's name did you find me?" he asked.

"Helga found me...then I met Eilina on the trail...I am sorry for Thor, Gundar."

"Helga?" A glimmer of hope sparked in Gundar.

"Come sit by the *fyr* with me and eat, Gundar," Skuli said, pulling out food from his pouch. "I have dried meat, cheese, berries," Skuli continued, wanting time to consider his words before speaking of Helga.

Gundar pulled himself up and sat down cross-legged opposite Skuli, near the *fyr* surrounded by dark night, the flames glowing on their faces.

"Venison," Skuli said, handing Gundar a piece of dry meat.

Gundar took it and bit into it.

"When I met Eilina," Skuli said, "she brought me back to Raumalen."

"Raumalen! She's not safe there," Gundar rushed to say.

"She would not leave her village, and it is only you they are looking for now," Skuli replied. "Here, she sends this." He handed Gundar his leather pouch.

"I paid her with trouble for all her kindness," Gundar said, placing the pouch inside his tunic.

"She does not think of it that way," Skuli said, pausing, knowing he had to speak about Helga. "Gundar, Helga told me that you would be needing help, to bring Lina back to her," he began, knowing Gundar would make his own sense of her words.

"Yes," Gundar said, understanding her meaning. "Lina..." knew Helga still held her heart apart from him.

Skuli saw it in Gundar's face. Gundar was hoping for more. "I think her heart still adrift," Skuli offered.

"Thor lives in Valhalla. He died as a warrior," Gundar said, as though speaking to Helga to soften her anger.

"The Gods know it," Skuli assured him.

"Would Helga," Gundar said, watching the flames. After a moment, he said, "I have heard tell of a new land. Beyond Iceland. Beyond Greenland. Bjarni

Herjolfson has seen it. Leifr Eiriksson goes to prove the tale."

Skuli nodded, not sure what to say.

Gundar looked at his friend and wanted to speak his heart.

"I dream of these things, if I live..." Gundar confessed, "...to bring Helga and Lina there." Gundar shook his head, adding, "But Skuli, this is not your fight, and I tell you, I think not to survive it in the end."

"It is not your thinking, but the gods, that will determine your fate. You will live, Gundar," Skuli said, speaking with the power of his life, and his love for Gundar. "The skein of my life is set with you, I always knew, and I will not lose the place Odin holds for me at his table when I repay my debt," he added good-naturedly.

Skuli's spirit was unshakeable and it strengthened Gundar, as did Skuli's loyalty, but he replied, "Nevertheless, I will not let you die for me."

"Eat. You will need your strength," Skuli said, handing him another piece of dried meat.

As Gundar took it and ate, Skuli reached into his pile of saplings, and pulled one out to begin stripping the bark with his sweord. He fashioned each end into a long spear point, and then began tapering the width on each end from the center.

"'You weaken it," Gundar observed.

"The southern seafarers showed me," Skuli answered, continuing to taper the point. When he was finished, he began hardening the points in the glowing coals.

As Gundar looked at him, he offered, "It will fly like a hawk, Gundar," knowing the odds were against them, but trying to keep his tone spirited. "Like a hawk."

Skuli took another stave from a pile.

"I will get Lina. You cannot run, and your force grows less," he said.

"You will not live," Gundar intoned.

"You will have to," Skuli said, as Gundar watched him fashioning the spear.

Skuli had always been the only man who could tell him anything and now Gundar knew he was offering his life in exchange for his daughter. "Skuli," Gundar began to say.

But Skuli interrupted, "In the morning, we ride!"

"Ride?" Gundar asked.

"Alaskr! Rudnar!" Skuli called, and two horses answered with their neighing.

"How?" Gundar asked, astonished.

"Eilina. From Mord, the blacksmith. The tale of the infant and the hawk spreads through the whole North Country. Now sleep, for in the morning we war, and our force cannot fail."

Gundar fell asleep thinking of Eilina and all that she had given him to help him save his daughter. He knew her spirit would be there with him when he went into battle, along with Helga's.

An hour before dawn, he walked away from the small *fyr* Skuli had been tending all night, and walked up the slope to a large clearing in the trees, where he looked into the sky.

Above him hawks were gliding. In intertwined circles, their wings motionless and outstretched, two red-tailed hawks rode the currents, rising higher, and

181

hunted. They rose above the filtered sunlight in the dark blue-green branches of the tall evergreens, higher into the clear blue ceramic of the northern sky.

It was said hawks mated for life, and somehow he knew these were together.

He could remember little of the weeks behind him. He only knew everything had brought him to this hour. It was all that he had left.

He heard footsteps behind him and turned to see Skuli coming to join him.

"They say hawks mate for life," Gundar said, still looking into the sky, not expecting an answer.

Skuli watched him for a moment.

"Today will be a hard fight, Skuli," Gundar said.

"But we'll be the stronger for it, Gundar," Skuli said, "so Valhalla can wait."

Gundar turned full round to Skuli, nodding, thankful for his courage, and meeting eyes to join his force with Skuli's, "Valhalla can wait."

* * *

Goth, confident his warriors would easily defeat King Olaf's men, now surveyed the scene at the cliffs of Trollveggen. He had made his decision.

He saw a warrior holding Lina at the cliff's edge, a second warrior beside him, and seven more standing guard. Shouting, "A river raid!" he rushed forward.

As the second warrior turned round to look down to the river four thousand feet below, Goth leaned his shoulder down and smashed into his back, launching him far into the air off the cliff to plummet screaming to his death.

Pulling his shortssword as he rose to his full height again, he sliced down on the arm that held Lina by the hand, severing it cleanly at the shoulder, then spun round and cleaved another rushing warrior at the waist. Lina screamed as the arm fell away and she lost her balance, beginning to fall over the cliff. Goth grabbed her as she fell, lifting her away from the cliff's edge, and then tossing her to safety.

As another warrior rushed him from the cliff side, he picked him up and threw him at the two other warriors so that the three of them fell from the high cliff, joining their companions far below.

He lifted Lina up in the crook of his arm to his shoulder and carried her off.

Lina looked up at him. "They were bad men," she said.

Goth nodded, touched by the child sharing her thoughts, still fearless, or uncomprehending, he did not know which. Then, to Goth's surprise, she kissed him on the cheek. Old emotions stirred in his heart, and conflicted with his blood feud against this child. "They did not hurt you?" he asked.

Lina shook her head. "Did they hurt you?"

Goth boosted her higher on his shoulder. "You will be safe in my lodge."

CHAPTER FIFTEEN
THE GAUNTLET

Gundar and Skuli galloped horses' hooves driving hard, leaning deep into the curving trails as the snow in the branches fell down upon them, churning up a white spray behind their horses. It was a new wind in Gundar's face, and he breathed it into his lungs with a renewed hope.

When they crested the ridge, they pulled their horses up short, looking down upon Goth's timber lodge below.

Their breaths heaved in their chest, mixing with the breath of the horses, filling the cold morning air with mist, as they surveyed the landscape from atop their horses.

Below, they saw a giant figure approaching the lodge, carrying a young child in his arms.

"She's alive!" Gundar exclaimed.

"Thank Odin!" Skuli added.

Gundar spun his horse around to a higher knoll, attempting to get a vantage point, resisting the urge to ride down upon them.

Skuli joined him, looking down at Gundar's leg. The wound had opened again on Gundar's thigh and his blood was running.

Skuli took out a small pouch and gave it to Gundar. "Put it under your bandage before battle. You will not feel that leg, but it will not last, not even for an hour."

Gundar spotted the deep cut of a ravine, winding back behind the lodge.

"You will have to circle the lodge," Gundar said, looking to the ravine. "Can you cross it?"

Skuli answered by whirling his horse around, "You will see me again!" He gave his horse a kick, yelling "Yaah!" and galloped down toward the ravine.

* * *

Gundar, sitting deep in his saddle, began slowly walking his horse down the trail. The certain rhythm of his horse's hooves on the hard ground hammered out a warning to men and gods alike. The sound echoed through the silent forest, returning to steady the rising pulse of blood etching his purpose into his veins.

He snapped the reins and his horse began to trot, as he moved with it, tuning his balance to the new rhythm.

He snapped the reins again, pushing his heels into his horse's flanks, so that it snorted and began to lope. It was then that he knew he rode no village beast. However Mord had come by him, this horse had been to war. This, too, the gods had given him.

Now with a shout and a hard kick, he drove his mount into a full gallop, leaning forward against its mane. A mile passed in a moment, his horse's hooves flying furious over the hard ground, as he descended into a hollow to rise again on the hill.

Now every labor of his breath and sense served the sweord-knowledge in his limbs as the approaching battle ignited his blood to fiery flames. He breathed that *fyr* as it breathed him, consuming all doubt and fear to burn white hot all the moments of his existence into a single flame that readied for battle the forge of his newborn soul.

This day, this hour, he would leave this world or return to another. Even as the shadows of doubt flew at him like the wolves of Raumalen, he joined his spirit to the task ahead, hardening his will, and making fierce his force. No enemy in this world could stop him now, or all the gods of Asgard. He leaned forward onto the horse's neck, feeling nothing but the wind and the hard driving muscles of his mount against his chest.

The first arrows fell upon him, and he began cutting his horse left and right to avoid the deadly rain. He drew his own bow, notched an arrow and shot, and shot again – the arrows flew true and ended those warrior's lives, as he rode on like a river of wind, like god's torrent in the high branches.

Rounding a bend, he saw two warriors posted on either side of a cleft in the hill. Without slowing his horse, Gundar again lifted up his bow, and notching one arrow after another, shot them both through the chest where they stood. They fell into the trail so his horse leapt over them as he flew past.

"Goth," he roared through the forest, knowing that with each turn of the trail he grew closer to killing his sworn enemy. Vengeance rang in his blood, his rage over Thor's killing riding first over and then alongside his will to save his daughter.

"Goth!" he roared again.

At the next bend, four warriors blocked the path. He came upon them as a gale, trampled two before he whirled round to battle the other two. He smashed the wooden shield of the first with a great downward blow and followed with another blow through the helmet. He pivoted his horse around and swung his sweord in a great swirling arc to cut the throat of the other.

"Goth!" Gundar thundered, filling the woods and the heavens above.

He galloped on, holding fierce to his reins, his horse's sweat growing thick on its back. Let his life be dust and his heart only the wind's brief twilight passage, if on that bridge between the worlds he might see the way to give Helga and Lina life.

* * *

Skuli estimated the chasm's expanse. Across the ravine, a warrior stood unaware, thinking himself protected by the distance. Counting his steps, Skuli walked back twelve paces. Then he began running towards the ravine, stopping short at the cliff's edge to let fly his spear. The warrior, alerted by his footsteps, turned to look closer just as the spear pierced his chest. He fell dead into the ravine.

Skuli picked up his remaining spears under his arm and began running again. He stopped to tie a stone to the end of a rope, and whipping it overhead, swung it over a strong tree limb on the far side. Gripping the rope tight, he jumped and flew through the air to a lower spot in the other side of the ravine. He dropped his spears as he landed, holding onto one to let it fly into the chest of the warrior who was running toward him.

He pulled his shortsweord in time to stab another attacking warrior through the heart, and then hack off the arm of another and slash his throat.

There was a moment of quiet. He counted four spears left. He climbed the ridge above the hut where they held Lena. The height would give his throwing an advantage.

He let the first fly in a great arc to pierce the side of a warrior.

Three more came running as he ran down the hill. Taking a spear in each arm, he rushed toward them, letting flying his spears one after another into their chests. When the third warrior reached him, he ducked his blow, and cut off his leg at the knee.

An archer took aim at him, but he launched his sweord to pierce his neck. With his last spear, he killed the last guard standing atop the hut. He leapt down upon the roof of the hut, and surveyed the ground around before grabbing the roof's edge to swing down through a window.

As he flew suddenly into the room, Lina cried, "No!"

A warrior burst in, shooting an arrow into Skuli's side. Skuli rushed him with his long knife as he tried to notch another arrow and drove his knife under his breastbone.

"Lina! Quiet! I come with your father!" he whispered,

Then he yanked at the arrow in his side, but it was in too deep. He broke it off at his rib cage.

He grabbed her under his arm and leapt out through the window.

* * *

Gundar galloped down the trail, bringing his sweord down first on a helmet, and then a shoulder, even as another warrior struck at his horse's legs, pitching him forward over his horse. He hit the ground still holding his sweord fast, rolling as the warrior struck at him, leaping to his feet and wielding a great downward two-handed stroke to cut through the helmet and shield of the first attacker, cleaving his chest. He sliced the throat of the next with a sideways slash of the knife he whipped from his belt. Without turning, he rammed his sweord back through the belly of the warrior rushing him from behind, and then deflected with his forearm a spear thrust at his chest. He killed that warrior with a blow down through his chest.

As he spun around, looking for more warriors, he heard laughter, a deep booming laughter that filled the forest, and then Goth's thundering shout, "Enough!"

Gundar, his breath roaring, strained to see Goth on the hill above through the trees and the sweat in his eyes.

"I see my father taught you well," Goth shouted.

Gundar surveyed the forest for a trap.

"Until you killed him," Goth continued.

"I killed him," Gundar shouted. "Or he would have killed me."

When finally his eyes focused, he saw Goth not thirty yards ahead, standing on the trail crest with the sun at his back, like a great tree blocking the sun. On either side of him stood six of his greatest warriors, all nearly as large as himself.

"Give me my daughter or you will all die," Gundar shouted.

Goth's warriors laughed. But even before they stopped laughing, faster than the eye could see, Gundar let fly two arrows, each hitting a warrior's shield at top dead center – they knew Gundar could have aimed higher.

Goth thundered at him, "Give me my father's scrolls!"

The scrolls, too, Gundar thought. More for Goth's anger.

"Take them yourself!" Gundar shouted back. "They blow across the ice lakes."

"Then your journey is over," Goth shouted, "because today you will you die."

Gundar heard Goth's words, listening to his own breath heaving in his chest even as he surveyed the trees around him for danger. He had to think, buy time, and fight against his own raging blood crying for Thor's vengeance, held fast now only by his hope of a future with Helga and Lina.

He shouted, "You hide behind a girl child, knowing your time of walking this earth is near an end."

"I will hang my sweord over my hearth with your blood still dripping!" Goth yelled back. "And boast to my grandchildren of your killing!"

Goth's men nodded, enjoying the ritual of insults before battle, waiting for Gundar's retort, but it was another voice that broke the silence –

CHAPTER SIXTEEN

REDEMPTION

"Father!" Lena's voice struck Gundar with the force of a stone hammer.

Goth and Gundar looked to the near eastern hill to see Skuli holding Lena by the hand. She was safe. Gundar's blood, released, ignited again, even as one of Goth's warriors appeared beside Goth, holding the reins of Skuli's horse.

Goth looked over again at Lina and she smiled at him, and Goth, at that moment, in all his anger and bitterness, and lifelong hatred, could not keep himself from smiling back.

Goth's warriors started to move toward Skuli, but Goth waved his hand. "Let them go. Or watch. I free them." Then he turned to Gundar and yelled, "Do you hear, Gundar? I free them! Throw down your bow, and I will come down to finish this."

Gundar heard Goth's words, while watching Goth's warriors. He tried to sense whether Goth was speaking the truth. He looked to Skuli and Lina, to Goth, to the sky, and back to Goth. He knew his decision would mean Lina's life or death.

"On your oath, Goth!" he yelled, throwing down his bow and then raising his sweord. "On your oath we will finish it!"

He rushed toward Goth with a roar.

Goth strode down the hill, sweord held high, and struck a great overhead blow. Gundar blocked it just above his head, holding his blade steady, while his metal held and rang over the hillside. Then, stepping to one side, he swung around to drive his sweord in a great arc towards Goth's back. Goth spun round and easily blocked Gundar's blow with the metal plate on his forearm.

"Here's no old man, Gundar," Goth scoffed.

The forest rang loud with the clash of their sweords, again and again, until, to all watching, their battle seemed to shake the very trees and loose the heavens above.

"This is the last music you'll hear," Goth boasted.

Their battle raged on, Goth the stronger but Gundar the faster, first Goth and then Gundar ruling the sweordplay as each seemed to grow stronger from their enemy's every blow.

Then suddenly, Gundar, with his sweord rebounding from a blocked thrust, swung his sweord overhead, and down, cleaving Goth's arm cleanly at the elbow. Goth reeled back.

"A fair blow, Gundar. That arm had itself severed many," Goth uttered, picking up his sweord in his left hand. "But we are far from finished."

Goth roared and struck such a fierce overhead blow it knocked Gundar back, and then struck again and again, the demon within him unleashed with his blood, until Gundar toppled back crashing to the ground against the roots of a tree. Goth raised his sweord for the killing blow. Lina screamed. Goth hesitated. Gundar rolled off the roots as Goth roared, "Die!" and crashed his sweord down into the tree.

Goth's sweord shook and Goth faltered, feeling himself weakening. Gundar saw it and leapt up, attacking. Swinging with a great overhead blow, he met Goth's raised sweord, rebounding from it and swinging down to slash Goth's right thigh, even as Goth's sweord slashed through his chain mail to slash his side. Goth fell.

Knowing it was over, Goth threw his sweord on to the ground.

"Send me now to join my father in Valhalla, Gundar, and you will have your vengeance."

Gundar raised his sweord for the kill, but then looked up the hill where his daughter was watching.

"Kill me!" Goth roared in a last cry, "Gundar, the great warrior..."

Gundar stared down at Goth, his blood running into the ground. Images of violence flashed before him, the sweord plunging through Thor's belly, Helga's hand on the knife into Thor's heart, Helga's anger toward him at the hut of arrows, all burning white-hot inside him, raging and reaching to possess his soul.

Yet now, as Gundar stood over him, his sweord held high, his breath and blood cooling, the man, Goth, appeared to him. He saw the man who had been born the boy he had once known. His hands gripped tight his sweord's hilt, his arms shaking over his head, as he wavered in his will. He met Goth's eyes, searching for the man he might destroy to have his vengeance. He found there instead, only a sorrowful, angry man who had lost those he loved. He found himself.

Goth waited for the killing blow, still staring defiantly into the eyes of his father's killer.

Gundar lowered his sweord.

He turned toward Goth's warriors still standing on the hill. "Your lord needs bandaging," Gundar shouted.

Goth's men stood frozen atop the hill.

Gundar turned and knelt down at Goth's side. With his sweord, he cut a piece of cloth from his tunic, and tied Goth's bleeding arm.

"I will grow another, Gundar, and find you," Goth said.

"You want to know of the scrolls, Goth? Know they saved your life today. Your hate has found you, but it will not find me, or my blood, ever again."

At that moment, both Goth and Gundar, as though in some silent understanding born of the war between them, looked to Lina, who stood afar, seeing them with a child's life-giving eyes, reflecting to them the sorrow that their lives had become in the emptiness of vengeance.

Then, as their eyes met for the last time, Goth and Gundar both knew, between them, it was finished, forever. Gundar stood and climbed the hill toward his daughter.

Goth's men ran to him as Gundar rushed to his daughter and Skuli. As he approached them, Skuli's knees buckled, and he fell to the ground. Gundar ran to kneel down at his side.

"Now, my friend, my debt is paid, and Valhalla cannot wait," Skuli said, struggling to smile.

Gundar saw Skuli's wound, and knew Skuli spoke true.

"Then go there, Skuli, my hearth-companion, and I will join you soon at Odin's table."

Skuli reached out to hold Gundar's upper arm. "She loves you still, Gundar. Seek her in Ravndal."

Then he fell back and was gone.

Gundar stood. Lina looked up to him and took hold of his hand.

A gust of wind shook the leaves from the branches overhead. Gundar watched them swirl down around him.

Then he made fast his leather pouch to his waist, and lifted Lina into his arms to climb the few yards to the ridge crest.

Dawn had fully broken, the sun's orange orb burning brightly atop the eastern mountains. To the west, over the distant ridges through the mountain breaks, the blue sea flew up into a silver-knifed sky.

Somewhere out there was the woman that was his life.

He began to walk down toward the sea.

To Helga, to a new world, perhaps to a new God.

END

www.ingramcontent.com/pod-product-compliance
Lightning Source LLC
Chambersburg PA
CBHW030312180626
46810CB00003B/1047